BACKSTEP FORWARD

F. Thomas Jones

authorHOUSE®

AuthorHouse™
1663 Liberty Drive
Bloomington, IN 47403
www.authorhouse.com
Phone: 1-800-839-8640

First published by AuthorHouse   1/27/2011

ISBN: 978-1-4520-8440-4 (sc)
ISBN: 978-1-4520-8441-1 (hc)
ISBN: 978-1-4520-8439-8 (e)

Library of Congress Control Number: 2010915699

Printed in the United States of America

This book is printed on acid-free paper.

To my parents, Gene and Fred,
with whom a trip backward would be both a pleasure and a privilege

Contents

Chapter 1: The Harvest

Mark Pickford was in a cheerful mood as he made his way among the furrows of the East Field. It was a beautiful morning, with sunlight pouring in through a large gap between two purplish mountains on the southwest horizon. The field was nestled safely on a plateau, firm and green, overlooking the quiet town in the valley below. The sun continued to inch upward into the sky, bringing with it all the hopes of those who would be coming that day. Mark paused and let out a sigh; no matter how many times he was greeted with this placid view, it never seemed to grow old. But then, here, nothing ever did.

He was a forty-four-year-old doctor, and had come to this place many years before. His work was certainly interesting, and extremely vital. He had developed a special "sense", which he possessed for as long as he could remember. That "sense" allowed him to adeptly traverse the field and harvest humans, pulling them right up out of the ground, as if they were common vegetables. These people were greeted by their families, who also had premonitions of the event that resulted in that new family member's time of arrival. Mark felt honored to be a part of the transition process for the entry of loved ones to this new world – a land of promise that produced a reversal of fortunes, and perfection in the end – for everyone.

Before beginning the day's workload, Mark thought about the huge disagreement he had with Terri, his partner. They both had been anticipating a special event, one that would certainly make Mark's job a lot easier, but they were at odds about how he should best handle the situation. Terri expressed her view that the orientation should be a quick one, so that the new doctor could go to work in the field as quickly as possible, after being harvested. Selfishly, she wanted to spend a lot more time with Mark – the last few days had been extremely busy ones; she had found herself becoming angry with the new doctor before he had even made his way to this place.

Mark, on the other hand, wanted to be as patient as possible with Evan, the associate who would be joining him shortly. The middle-aged doctor rubbed the course whiskers on his chin and gazed up at the shimmering white clouds, billowing high in the sky. As he noticed the silver-gray outline, he chuckled to himself. The once-similar color that sketched across his jaws was becoming less and less gray all the time. He was aware of the fact that his muscles didn't seem to ache nearly as much in the mornings as they used to. He wondered what he might do to occupy his time when he grew younger, if not for his own arduous, emotion-packed occupation. Perhaps he would fish, or maybe he would just gaze up at the warm sky and daydream about clouds and trees and the games that children play.

Just as he started to become pre-occupied with thoughts of bliss, Mark was suddenly snapped back in to reality as his "sense" (which he referred to as the "East Field Tingle", or EFT) began to kick-in once again. He walked toward one of the center furrows, where he was greeted by three familiar faces – that of a dark-haired woman (about his age) and an elderly couple. As he approached, a nervous smile appeared on the woman's face. Words did not come easily for any of them, although they all shared a most unique bond. The reason they were all gathered was clear; the importance of the moment was about to be revealed.

The doctor's steel-blue eyes looked into the emerald glint of the attractive lady. Her hair cascaded past one side of her face, shadowing some of her worried wrinkles. The woman's name was Adelaide ("Addy", for short). Standing just behind her left shoulder, the two older people nudged closer, supporting her with their collective weight. All three seemed fairly calm, but Mark could tell they were all apprehensive about what was about to happen there in the center of the field.

"Are you ready for this, Addy?" he asked carefully. Then, he glanced at the elderly couple – "Folks, you know the drill, right?" Without a word, they nodded and tried to look elsewhere; they did not want the doctor to see the tears that were forming on their faces. He was about to say something of comfort to the couple, but his attention suddenly shot back in Addy's direction as she hit him directly with a question.

"Mark, what kind of shape will he be in when he arrives?"

"I'm not going to lie to you. It will be pretty traumatic at first," he pointed out. "Remember all those things we talked about, earlier?"

"Yes, I remember …"

"You've got to give Evan time to get adjusted," he said, "and I just don't know how long that's going to take."

The older man and woman looked at each other, then they looked down and began to uncomfortably shuffle their feet, in obvious agitation. They remained silent, but continued to have a grip on Addy's arm and shoulder – in part to support each other, but perhaps to help keep her steady, as well.

Addy shook her head and bit her lower lip. "For Evan's sake, I hope it doesn't take long."

"For ALL of our sakes!" interjected the older man, with a wry grin. "Mark, you need the help a lot worse than I do!" Walter, the old man, was trying to make light of the fact that he would have to assume responsibility for Evan during his arrival and the first few days of transition to his new life and his new family. Walter clearly understood that he would have to bear much of the early burden on his own. Yet, he didn't seem to mind.

"Just trust me everyone, okay?!" Mark tried to offer some last words of reassurance as he instructed the three people to turn their backs to him, while he completed the procedure he knew so well.

"You may hear some disturbing things, but I don't want any of you to worry. Evan will be in a dream-like state; he will not know or recognize anything or anyone, at first. Don't take anything he says at face value, and please don't take anything too personally. He's going to be pretty messed-up for a little while."

Addy, Walter, and Margaret all joined hands and turned away from Mark, as he had told them to. Just then, beneath their feet, the ground started to tremble. The semblance of a human cranium began to emerge from the soil.

"He's coming! Warren, get over here quick!" Mark barked instructions and motioned feverishly for his young associate to join him in the center of the field. Warren, a young man of about eighteen years of age, rushed over with some clean towels and a long purple cloak. "Is this the one you've been telling me about?" he asked.

"Yes, he is the one. Any impressions you may have of him during these next moments will go away after a week, so don't worry. Just hand me the towels and be ready for my next set of instructions".

The doctor and his young protege began easing the male form out of the ground. As the tortured, contorted figure began to moan, Mark turned his head and yelled over his shoulder toward Addy and the two individuals steadying her.

"Start singing the song that we have been working on," he said. "Sing it as softly and sweetly as you can, and try your best to ignore everything that you hear coming from Evan's mouth."

"Is he all right?" Addy asked. "I need to know!"

"Everything will be just fine," Mark said. Though his words sounded confident enough, deep down he hoped that indeed things would work out just the way he said they would. The three people sang in unison, as Warren and Mark carefully and dutifully freed Evan from his subterranean tomb.

The sound of the carefully-rehearsed melody was interrupted by Evan's agonizing cry. It was incoherent at first, but Addy suddenly stopped singing when she heard her name.

"What's happening?" she yelled toward Mark, now almost in a panic. "He's calling my name. He needs me ... now!"

"We discussed this before," Mark tried to reassure her. "That would not be a good idea!"

"Good idea or not, he needs me and I am not going to turn my back on him any longer!" With that, Addy wheeled around and gasped in horror. The face seemed vaguely familiar, but it was distorted with fear and anguish. The body was gaunt and curled in an awkward fashion. "Could this really be Evan?" she thought.

Mark thought this had been a pretty typical delivery -- nothing spectacular. Addy, unsure of what exactly was going on, clutched the shaking body of the man she had waited for all these many years. She stroked his forehead and bathed his face with tears of both joy and relief. "I'm right here, my love", she whispered. "I'm right here".

It had been cold and dark – the silence that swirled around him made him intensely fearful. And yet, Evan could faintly hear the pounding pulses coming from somewhere above. His mind struggled to grasp a thought – where he was; how he felt; but he could not focus on any one particular thing. He believed that his eyes were open, and yet he could see nothing. Trying desperately to raise his hand before his face, he found himself immobile; trapped. The sound of a rustling wind spiraled into his ears and he felt drunk with dizziness. Just as he began to succumb to the notion of terrifying despair, he felt a light breeze around the top of his head.

As it grew steadily, he felt himself being pushed upward. It was so very strange, almost as if some magical force was propelling him. The torrent of wind gradually calmed, feeling neither warm nor cold … simply peaceful. The noises he had heard became a little less muffled. He heard a voice scream; then a barrage of thunder exploded around him. It was all so confusing! Evan felt two pairs of strong hands grip the hair on his head and both sides of his skull. They began to pull upward, ever so gently. He felt the sensation of warm light bathing his face, but he still could not see.

He found himself totally helpless, and at the mercy of his strange captors. The voices he heard sounded as if they were faint echoes down a long, narrow corridor. They seemed almost familiar, but his mind was still a blur. He felt the rest of his body being carefully pulled out of the ground. It was gently laid out and covered; then the voices tapered away and left him in silence. Evan's mind continued to wander in a ghostlike state. For a moment, he thought that he heard the sounds of a small choir, directly above him. The music soothed and calmed him, and he was carried off into a feeling of euphoric peace, shrouded in enchantment. His fear melted away into a deep sleep.

When he finally opened his eyes, Evan's gaze met with a pair of piercing green eyes, nestled into the delicate features of a beautiful, tear-stained face. Addy stroked his hair lovingly, as she delicately uttered the words:

"Welcome home, dear".

He *knew* her – he knew her face, her smile, her voice, everything about her. But how could this be possible? As his eyes continued to focus, Evan weakly blurted out: "Is it really you, Addy?" He was confused as the words came out of his mouth – he didn't know where they came from, or what provoked them. He had no idea why he said the name, and he became fearful once again. All he could do was stare up into her face, as his eyes continued to adjust to the light, and as he waited for what she might say in return. Two loving eyes looked upon him; as she nodded her head, and a single tear drifted down one cheek and got caught in the crease of her emerging smile.

"Your Addy is right here; and I've been waiting for you", she whispered.

Evan made one final, desperate attempt to speak; words formed in his throat, but were choked off by both his brain and his fear. Addy put two fingers gently across his lips and calmly suppressed his attempts to say what his mind was struggling to put into words.

"Shhhhhh-hhhhh … rest for awhile. Just know that I am right here with you and that things will be much better in a couple of days."

His brain enveloped the voice and cradled the words. What could she possibly mean by that? How would a couple of days make anything any better – any different? Wearily, as he began to drift off to sleep once again, the peace he had felt before was now giving way to a mysterious and intense anger. He battled the sleep demons as he tried to figure out why he was suddenly becoming filled with rage. Evan couldn't understand the chain of events that were unfolding: nothingness, followed by cold and dark; then, being jerked up out of the ground and peacefully laid flat – all accompanied by beautiful singing, the face of a woman … all giving way to a foaming rage. What could all this mean, and what caused it all in the first place? All that he knew was that his name was Evan; but, as he was losing consciousness, even that became a mettlesome blur in his conflicted and confused state.

Suddenly, his eyes flashed open. His own wild look was greeted by another face, but this one did not belong to Addy. As he began to focus, he made out the shape of someone who appeared to be about his own age and build. This stranger had a caring gleam in his steel blue eyes and a very careful, yet firm, touch. His hands pressed warmly around the tops of Evan's shoulders, and a smile broke out across his face as the newcomer's cobwebs began to clear.

"Welcome back, old chum!" the man bellowed out, in a hearty tone.

Instantly (although Evan did not know how), he was able to recognize the man and the voice. It was Mark Pickford. But how did he know this? More and more, Evan was baffled by the way bits of knowledge were flooding back into his brain, and he battled to make sense of it all.

"I wondered when you might finally come around", the doctor said. "Just take your time, and let me know when you're ready, because we've got plenty of work ahead of us today."

Evan carefully processed the words and he thought as hard as he could. What kind of work was this man talking about? None of this was making any sense! He shut his eyes tight, trying hard to remember. Then, almost immediately, the answer came to him, like a bolt of lightning.

Why, of course! Mark (who was also known to many as "Dr. P") was his colleague (though it must have been in a former life). No, wait! Dr. P was in the business of harvesting souls. Just then, it occurred to him that he himself had just been harvested. If this was indeed the case, how in the world could they be colleagues? His thoughts continued to be cloudy. All he wished for was the sight and the touch of Addy. Although he couldn't remember who she was exactly, he strongly felt as if she could be the one person who might be able to bring some sort of order to his now-chaotic existence ...

"Unless she had merely been a dream!" he suddenly thought. Horrified by these new prospects, another strange notion slammed against the confused chasm he was submerged in: he seemed to recall that a period of fogginess was prevalent for about twenty-four hours after a person had been harvested. That would at least explain all the crazy feelings he was having, and the fact that he could make no sense of each new revelation that creeped into his brain. He looked up at the face of the re-assuring doctor, who gave him a warm smile and said, somewhat in a rush, "Now, let me begin to tell you all the things you have to do today".

As he heard these words, Evan felt the scary sensation of fury begin to build up inside him once again -- markedly different from the calm and serenity he had felt when the music of the beautiful singing voices had carried him off into dreamland. This was the same feeling he had remembered, right before he had fallen asleep, holding Addy's hand. It was an uncontrollable rage – he didn't know what caused it, or what might make it go away. He felt consumed with outrage and aggression, and yet he still couldn't figure out why.

"Where's Addy?" he snapped. Dr. P looked almost as if he had been expecting this kind of outburst. As he leaned down next to the patient's right ear, he slowly and authoritatively said, "It's time for you to get up. There's someone that you have to meet". Although Evan was angry, he knew for some reason that he had to comply with the doctor's request.

"Are you taking me to see Addy?" he asked firmly. As soon as the words exited, he knew for some reason that the answer would be "No", and this made him absolutely seethe.

Dr. P simply shook his head as he helped Evan slowly to his feet and steadied him for his next destination. He was very curious about the hostility welling up from deep within this man's soul.

As he gained confidence in his steps, Evan looked toward Mark again and asked the one question that his caretaker had hoped to avoid:

"Can you tell me why I am so angry?"

Mark stopped for a moment, gently slapped him on the back and looked him squarely in the eyes. "I can't tell you exactly, but the person who I am taking you to see will answer a lot of your questions. In fact, after you spend some time with him, you'll finally be ready to come to work."

"But when will I see Addy?!" the patient clamored, rather obstinately. This time he raised his voice a lot more forcefully. Dr. P, trying his best to dismiss it without getting angry himself, took a deep breath, and pointed to a hill on the eastern horizon.

"You will see Addy again; I promise. But right now, we need to go over there", he said, as he pointed again toward a gently rising hill, which was blanketed in a deep green because of the cloud cover. "Before we can do anything else", he continued, "you need to come around 'full circle'. Only Walter can help you do that."

Walter! The name sounded oddly familiar to Evan, though he didn't know why. His anger mounted, because (right now) he didn't feel like he knew much of anything – except that he desperately wanted to see Addy again.

Chapter 2: The Old Man On The Hill

Dr. P guided Evan along the roughly-hewn path, around a large rock, to an expansive clearing. The sky was a brilliant blue, and there were several soft, puffy white clouds high overhead. The air was warm, and a slight breeze (reminiscent of the one that wafted over the top of Evan's head, as he was being harvested), passed by. Through the brightness, he saw in the distance a smoothly rounded hillside, dotted with pink and purple wildflowers. Seated on the hill, in neat little rows, were young children – most likely between the ages of two and six. Nestled among the children and the flowers was a frail, wrinkled old man. Evan guessed that this man must be Walter. As he approached, he studied the old man's features. There was something oddly familiar about him, although he had no way of knowing that Walter had been present when he had been pulled out of the ground just hours before.

"By the way, where exactly *are* we?" Evan wondered aloud. "Well, I thought you might *never* ask the question", chortled the doctor. "You have arrived at a place we call *Backstep*. I would tell you more, but that's why I am taking you to Walter. He will answer all your questions ... well, *most* of your questions. He is one of the most intelligent men in all the land. The children absolutely love him! You'll soon see why."

Evan diverted his attention to the old man. Walter wore a dingy, tan-colored robe and held on to a long staff (which, Evan surmised, he used as a walking stick). Leaning against a rock, one that was just big enough to bear his weight while his feet remained firmly planted on the ground, he edged slightly forward against the gnarled stick. Evan observed that as the man spoke, every child was extremely attentive. He also noticed that several adults had come to join the children on the hill. They were people just like himself; and many were clothed exactly the same, wearing long purple tunics and loose-fitting burlap pants.

As he studied his surroundings, Evan did his best to fight off his anger; he now understood that Mark was just trying to get him used to his new life.

"I can sit and listen for a little while, but then I've got to be on my way", he told his friend.

"Where do you have to go?" Evan questioned. But as soon as he said the words, he knew exactly where his new friend had to go -- back to the harvesting field. That was Dr. P's job – to harvest more people. Somehow, Evan knew that he would also be returning very soon to the same place, although he wasn't exactly sure how he knew, or why this was to be his destiny. He remembered that Mark had mentioned something earlier about getting him back to work, but he neither knew what that meant or exactly where it would be; right now, he was just guessing. However, the more he thought about the field, Evan felt like it was pulling him closer, like a protective mother pulls in her child.

As the two men sat and listened to the stories of the old man on the hill, Evan studied the face intently. Yes, indeed there was something strangely familiar about the voice, wrinkled face and hands, and even the crooked old staff. He started to ask a question, but Mark politely shushed him, as Walter continued his story:

"…*no one before had ever operated such a machine. It was made of the strongest steel and it was powered by a ferocious engine. But Davy was not afraid, and he continued to apply pressure to the lever. Slowly, the huge arm bent toward the ground and plunged the large shovel deep into the earth. But this was no ordinary shovel – No! It was massive, and could not be used by ordinary human hands. This kind of shovel could not only dig, but it could also tunnel in either direction. Can you imagine such an instrument?!*"

Mark pointed over toward a young boy, seated to the right of Walter, whose eyes were ablaze. The boy confidently smiled whenever the old man said the name Davy.

"The boy is amazed that the hero of this story is also named Davy", whispered Dr. P. "But what he doesn't know is that this story actually happened – happened to *him*."

"But how is that possible?" Evan quietly argued. Mark calmly lifted his hand to silence the protests of his friend.

"Walter has a unique gift; a gift that is possessed by every individual over eighty years of age. These people are too old and frail to work, but they are able to tell stories. The stories that they tell are about the very people they are telling the stories to – they are of things that have already happened. I have been told I also did this – many, many years ago."

Evan scratched his head in confusion, as Dr. P continued.

"The most amazing thing is that the audience has no knowledge or recollection whatsoever that their lives are being replayed, in story form. All they know is that they are being entertained."

"That just doesn't make any sense at all", Evan whispered. "How could these things have already happened, if they are only children? And even if they did, wouldn't they at least remember some of the details? And how is it that Walter knows all these things, anyway?"

Mark shook his head, in an effort to silence his friend. There were so many questions, and there was so much he wanted to be able to say. But time was ticking, and the doctor was needed back at the harvesting field. Mark could feel his own patience beginning to wear thin.

The two men sat down on the cool grass, behind all the children. Evan noticed that, periodically, other adults were coming and going. The ones who were just arriving seemed a lot more bewildered than the ones who were leaving. He observed that every adult who departed had an escort. He didn't realize what significance this might have, and he wondered who might come to lead him, when the time came for him to leave. Could it be Walter, perhaps?

As he continued to listen to Walter speak, things became clearer. After a few minutes, Mark got up from his grassy spot.

"I must leave you now; but when Walter finishes, you must go up and speak to him. He knows you and has been expecting your arrival today."

"I STILL don't understand!" Evan protested. He tried to fight off the anger that had started to grow once again.

"Oh, you will ... trust me", Mark offered. "Over the course of the next day or two, Walter will answer most of your questions and put your mind at ease. Then, I hope to see you back at the field."

As soon as he uttered the words, Evan's mind flashed back to the harvesting field. He knew right then what his job was; he just didn't know how we would be able to do everything that might be required of him.

Evan started to speak, but Dr. P interrupted –

"I've probably said too much already. I know it's all really confusing, but things will clear up before you know it ... oh, and all that anger will go away, too."

"But what about Addy?" Evan pleaded. "When will I see her again?"

"You will see her after the next dip of the sun, my friend. But, for now, you need to wait for Walter to finish his story and then accompany him to his house. After all, someone needs to see that the old man doesn't get into any trouble on the way home!"

When he said this, Mark cast a furtive smile and a wink in Walter's direction, then saluted him and turned around to make his way past the large rock. Walter's eyes gleamed and he winked back as he watched the doctor fade into the distance, never losing track of his place in the story he was telling to the throng that was gathered around him.

"Please, oh please, tell us another story, Mr. Walter!" Davy pleaded.

"All right, all right", said the old man. "I have one more story to tell, before I must go. This one starts out a little sad, but then it has a happy ending.

"Oooh, I like those", said one of the little girls seated in the middle of the group. "Those are the *bestest* kind!"

The old man arched back and allowed his eyes to meet up with Evan's. "There once was a man named … Evan".

A chill ran down the back of the man who wore the purple cloak. Suddenly, Evan's mind was riveted; the anger vanished, he now concentrated intently on the sound of the voice and the images that were to be revealed. After hearing his own name, he was sure that this story was about him, and that it would play some significant role in allowing him to find out more about himself and what his purpose was to be, in this new life that had been thrust upon him.

"If this is a story about me, it must have already happened," he began to reason.

"But if I have just arrived, how can that possibly be?"

He could not answer his own questions, and his curiosity gradually won the battle over his angst. He settled back on the grassy bank, and finally allowed Walter's words to enter his ears, and soak into his soul.

Chapter 3: Trying To Make Sense Of It All

The old man made sure that he had Evan's complete and undivided attention before he began. Children, and even adults, began to edge forward, eagerly anticipating the tale that was about to unfold. Evan found himself leaning in, as well. Walter slowly began:

Now you must understand, Evan came from a far-away place. When he first arrived, he was very angry, but he didn't know what he was angry about. For two days he did his job, and said mean things. People wondered if he was a nice person or not, because even though the job he was doing was helping others, he didn't seem at all happy. But then, the most amazing thing happened ..."

"What happened, what happened?!" squealed one of the children. The other children, and even some of the adults, laughed. Evan felt a bit of a smile poke through on his own face. But Walter's story was confusing. Could this *amazing thing* he was getting ready to talk about possibly have something to do with Addy? He almost blurted out the question, but something deep within him resisted. Things on the hill began to settle, and Walter started up once again:

"Yes, yes, my dear, it's all very exciting ..."

As much as Evan wanted to hear the man's story, his mind began to drift toward Addy once more. He remembered her touch, the way she looked, the words that she had said to him. He longed to be with her, and he didn't think he could wait another second. Certainly, the story that Walter was telling was about how the two of them would soon meet and sweep away all his anger. But then his mind recoiled: Hadn't she said that she would see him tomorrow? And if that was true, why would this have not been enough to appease him? Maybe the story wasn't about Addy at all! By the time he had re-focused his attention on Walter, most of the story had been told. Now, Evan was angry with himself for letting the moment pass.

A little girl named Allison spoke up: "It's so nice to get presents. Did Evan like the present that he got?"

"Oh yes, very much", Walter beamed. "In fact, he always said that it was one of the best presents he ever received. Well, that and maybe one or two others."

The children started laughing again. Walter clapped his hands twice and leaned forward:

"Now children, I'll see you all right back here tomorrow. I've got some more wonderful stories to tell you".

"We love you, Walter!" the young ones cried out, some in unison. As they each found an older person to take by the hand, to be led off, Evan noticed that some of the older people walking hand-in-hand with a few of the children were also wearing purple cloaks. This seemed very odd to him. Before he could try to make sense of it, Walter beckoned with his eyes for Evan to make his way forward. Obediently, the younger man did as the older one's stare instructed him to do. As he did, he noticed all the adults were now paired up with other, much older people. It dawned on him that Walter was the person who would now lead him to wherever the next place happened to be. Now, Evan was really upset with himself that he hadn't paid closer attention to the story!

Walter seemed to realize Evan's despair. He slowly pushed himself away from the rock and said, "Evan, please grab my arm. We have a bit of walking to do."

He was momentarily stunned. "How exactly do you know me?" Evan pondered. "You seem to know a great many stories. I just want to know *three* things: First of all, what is my relationship with Mark? Second, who in fact is this Addy woman? And the last thing I'd like to know is about this special present I'm supposed to receive."

Walter suddenly lurched forward against his stick; Evan thought he was about to fall, so he cinched his arm tightly; but the old man quickly regained his balance and his composure. "This is a confusing time for you", Walter confided. "However, I can promise you that between now and the next dip of the sun you will have a much clearer perspective of things. I think you'll even be ready to go to work!"

As the two men talked, they carefully worked their way around a jagged path, in the opposite direction from where Evan and Mark had originally come. Evan thought aloud once again: "I believe I remember Mark saying that the name of this place is *Backstep*. Can you tell me a little about this place? Maybe that would help me right now more than anything."

Walter stopped for a moment and stared into the younger man's eyes. "I can't tell you everything. But I will equip you with all the knowledge you need to help get you through the night."

"Is there anything particular about tonight I need to know or worry about?"

"You will have an extended dream that will last through the entire night. It will be a vivid recollection of the journey that brought you to this place. After that, you will have a different dream, which you will also have more than once - maybe for a few nights, weeks, months, maybe even years. This dream will be the one that holds your significance to this world in its grasp. Eventually, it will leave you and never revisit you again in the night. Once it is done, your dreams will then be able to take you anywhere —except for where you have already been."

"What you also need to know right now is that you have arrived here at the equivalent age of 42, and from here forward you will live your life backwards. When you wake up tomorrow, you will be one day younger. You will also be one day closer to perfection."

"*Backstep* is a very unique place. No one is born here, and there are no deaths. Your arrival coincided with a death somewhere else. When you were harvested, there were people around you, close to you, who already knew of you and were prepared for your arrival. I was one of those people … and so was Addy."

"Each day that you live, you will lose a little bit of your collective knowledge. Eventually, you will become a child; in due time, you will be a helpless infant. That is one of the reasons why you are with me now."

This rush of information was more than Evan could take in all at once. He stopped and cupped his hands over his face, and bent toward the ground.

"I simply don't understand" he wailed. "This contradicts any shreds of knowledge I have!"

"Not to worry", Walter reassured him. "Once we get you to my home and we get some food in you, I can prepare you for the next step of your journey. Why look —we're nearly there now."

Evan looked ahead and saw a stone hut with light smoke curling out of a makeshift chimney, leaning from one side of the roof. It looked sturdy, yet quite small.

"I will introduce you to Margaret. She and I will be your overseers, until the day you are finally taken from this place, forty-two years from now."

"Does that mean you two are my parents?" Evan asked delicately.

"You might think of it that way" Walter said. "Since there are no biological reproductions here, there are no actual parents like in the world that you came from.

But Margaret and I are your lifetime caregivers, and we will both be with you for the rest of your life here in *Backstep*."

"But what about Addy: is she kind of like - my wife? It's almost as if I know her; as if she has always been a part of me".

"In a way, she has been", Walter began to explain. "You see, just as Margaret and I are your lifelong guardians, Addy is your designated soulmate. You and Addy will have other people to care for, too. There are no formal marriages; no husband and wife, like in your old world ... only partnerships.

"What do you mean?" Evan burst forth. "I just got here, and now you tell me I have two caregivers who aren't my parents, a partner who isn't my wife, and people I have to care for who I don't even know about yet?!" Evan felt his blood begin to boil and he angrily stomped his foot. He reached down, picked up a rock and heaved it as hard as he could away from the hut, while letting out a horrifying scream of pent-up anguish and frustration. "And how come *you* know so much?!" he bellowed.

Walter stopped to gather his wits about him. Evan could tell that his patience had just about run out, but they both knew that he still had many questions that needed to be answered. After all, hadn't the old man intimated that he had to prepare Evan for what would prove to be a long and difficult night?

As they arrived at the front door of the hut, Walter raised a hand toward the younger man. "You must promise me one thing, Evan: try not to ask a lot of questions tonight. I will tell you a little about your dream, although I cannot give you specific details. You will have to fill me in tomorrow morning – as much as you are able to remember. Tomorrow, we will deal with your anger, and we will go see Addy."

As soon as the old man mentioned Addy's name, Evan's entire demeanor changed. His rage seemed to melt into a rush of warmth and timidity. He felt the need to immediately apologize for some of the caustic things he had said.

"I'm sorry for my temper, Walter. I just don't know why I am so angry."

"I suspect you will find clues about that during the course of your dream. Whatever it is, I am sure we will both be glad when it eventually goes away. And it will; please know that. Here, in *Backstep*, everything eventually leaves; but when it does leave, it becomes perfect!"

"Yeah, right! Some kind of perfection ... living your life backwards! I've never heard of anything so ridiculous!"

Walter countered: "Well, Evan, if you really think about it – it makes total and complete sense. In the place that we all arrive here from, life is not perfect – far from it! But when we arrive here, we re-trace the steps of our former lives (with some adaptations), until we are truly perfect beings. We are then taken off into the bright light of ever-lasting peacefulness. Tomorrow, before we go see Addy, I will take you to the place where the light carries away all the perfect little ones".

"Will it take away my anger, too?" Evan questioned.

"Your anger will eventually go away, though I'm not sure exactly when. Like I said, perhaps your dream will shed some light on that. We'll sit down and discuss it in the morning ... after you have had a nice, long sleep."

"I'm almost afraid to go to sleep now. How can I even think about sleeping, with all the things now weighing upon my mind?"

"Just come inside", Walter re-assured him. "The hour is growing late; the sun has almost dipped, and it is about time for some of Margaret's hot tea. It will relax you and help you sleep tonight."

"May I ask how long you and Margaret have been together ... as, uh, partners?"

"We have been together for about three years" Walter said. "That means we have a great many years ahead of us, to spend together."

"Why have you only been together for three years?' asked Evan.

Walter looked at him and cast a broad smile. He then said:

"Margaret has only been here for three years!"

Chapter 4: Dreams Last

It was clear upon Evan's arrival that Margaret had been expecting him. He sensed that she wanted to reach out and hug him, but she simply cast a sincere smile his way and said, "Welcome to our home." She had a light dinner prepared for him. The guest promptly and politely ate his fill, but very few words were spoken. It appeared as though Evan had many things to chew on other than the food. Across the table from him, Walter studied his every move, his arms crossed and a slight scowl wiped across his face. The old man was deep in thought himself.

After what seemed an interminable amount of time, Walter began to give Evan some instructions:

"Now, when you go to sleep tonight, do not be afraid of the visions you will have. Get used to them, because you will revisit them every night for the next several nights: every color, every detail, every moment. They will unlock the secret of your journey to this place. After that, you will have other dreams, which also have significance. I don't recall all the contents of my original dream; the one I have now is the only one I can vividly remember. Margaret's first dream has long faded, too; she has had a loop of varying dreams that have repeated every night for the past three years."

As he made this comment, Margaret closed her eyes and nodded her head. She finally spoke:

"You'll get used to the dream. You will also have an opportunity to share it with others. All people do, before the seventh night. The dream needs to be shared with the Council of Dreams, before it vanishes forever".

She stopped speaking and extended a warm mug to Evan. "Here, drink this hot tea. It will ease your mind, and help you to sleep better."

Evan took the mug from his host. The strong smell of the herbal concoction crawled up his nasal passages, enticing him to drink. He took one sip. Although it was a little on the pungent side, the taste was very smooth and a little sweet. Walter continued to study his guest as he drank the tea. He tried to make conversation, but was beginning to feel a little tired. He looked toward Walter, but the man's face seemed to elongate and slant to one side. Evan shook his head and looked again. Now, the old man leaned forward a little bit and asked "Are you feeling alright?" Evan thought that he heard the words, but they were in a much lower, distorted pitch and seemed to be spoken in slow motion. The room began to spin and he realized that he had been drugged. He got up from his chair, made it halfway to the bed in the corner, then collapsed. His body just barely made it onto the surface of the mattress. Both Walter and Margaret were thankful that they did not have to do any heavy lifting. Evan was out before his head even hit the pillow.

When he opened his eyes, Evan wasn't in the hut anymore. The scenery had changed; it was darker and much more sinister. The noise of heavy machinery surrounded him. He had on a black leather jacket, a pair of faded jeans and old black boots, covered with dust. He looked at himself in a mirror; the face, unshaven, sported a light growth of a brownish beard. Overall, he had a rather sloppy, unkempt appearance. Over and above everything else, however, he was angry.

He was standing in a hospital waiting room, peering through the glass at a young boy, only twelve years of age. Smoke curled around him as he tried to focus on the little face, which was hooked up to monitors and a breathing tube. He heard Addy's voice calling out his name, but he couldn't see her anywhere. All that he heard was the constant beeping of the heart monitor and a string of incoherent words coming at him from every direction.

"Cancer … poor kid … so young … cancer … no hope … no cure … senseless waste … so young … so young … gone."

He heard the long continuous beep of the monitor. Just then, he noticed that an unknown hand was reaching to pull the sheet over the boy's face. Evan suddenly realized it was his own son, Craig. Now he realized why he was so angry. He had just lost his son, a twelve year-old boy, to cancer. He could do nothing – only stand there and watch as the boy was taken away from him. And there stood Evan: a doctor, unable to do anything. He was a man whose business it was to heal others, yet he could do nothing to save his own son. Angrily, he stormed out of the hospital, as the smoke continued to swirl around him. From a distance, he could hear Addy's voice calling:

"Evan, Evan, where are you? Please come back to me! Don't do this! Don't do this!"

"Don't do *what*?" the doctor thought. "Who the hell cares what I do? I just lost my son!"

He stormed out of the hospital, in the middle of a driving rain. He got onto his motorcycle, and started to ride. As he made his way along the darkened streets, the sense of loss made the wrath fume deep inside him. The motorcycle passed a bar, then doubled back. Evan thought that perhaps he could find some small degree of solace in the bottom of a whiskey bottle.

The place was suitably named *The Red Light*. Evan parked his bike about fifty feet from the entrance, and slogged his way inside. Upon entering, he cast angry glances around the room, before sauntering up to the bar. He pounded a soaking wet, flat hand onto the top of the counter and shouted at the bartender:

"Whiskey! Give me a bottle of poison! Tonight, I'm going to kill it!"

The bartender eased his way over; he had seen this sight many times before: lonely, angry people, seeking to find comfort by drowning their sorrows in alcohol. Too many times he had heard stories of lives shattered, yet he continued to pour out what the patrons requested. Sometimes he wondered to himself:

"Why do I do this? Who am I *really* serving here?"

Evan quickly brought his server back into reality when he snatched the bottle away from him and began to pour himself a full glass. The man stared at Evan for a moment, as the patron raised his glass and loudly shouted: "To hell with life!" As he drank the entire glass in just two gulps, he could hear the echo of laughter from the dark recesses of the room. He looked around to see who might be the cause (or the blame), but he could see no other faces ... only the forms and shadows of bodies. Everyone seemed the same, as if there were no individuals here; just tortured souls, like himself.

The alcohol seemed to take effect very quickly; Evan felt his speech start to slur. The intoxicated man began to talk out loud, although the words he spoke were not very coherent.

His words mixed in with the laughter that bounced about the room, and his head began to swirl. Added to all this was his mounting feeling of total disregard for life. Suddenly, a new sound began to emerge and take root in his consciousness. It was the voice of a woman. It was saying, "Please don't do this … Where are you? … Please don't … No … No …" He knew the voice: it belonged to Addy. But where was she?

"Oh well, who cares, anyway? Certainly not me!" he thought aloud.

No matter – as long as he had his liquid poison and his anger to keep him company; that was all he needed. Evan knew that his newfound partner, rage, would not let him down, and would not abandon him. It would be his constant companion, and he would do his part to make sure it stuck around for the ride.

He lost track of time, and the whiskey bled from the bottle … and from the glass.

The words he spoke (though he still couldn't understand them), took on a more surly tone. Before he knew what was happening, he had gotten up from his stool and made his way toward the door. The bartender started to come out from behind the bar, perhaps in an effort to intervene and prevent his patron from leaving. As the bartender walked around, Evan suddenly stopped, and without even looking, slowly raised his arm and pointed a finger. "Don't even think about it!" he warned.

The man froze. Evan took one long last look at him, then turned and made his way out into the rain, which had seemed to pick up a little (or maybe that was just his imagination). He got on his bike, fired up the engine, and cried out to his new best friend and companion, "Okay, where to now?" His anger pointed him south, going nowhere in particular. He then sped off into the night.

As he rode, his mind seemed to become clearer. His rage spoke to his brain:

"You don't need these people. Every day, you work to save lives … those of people who don't even deserve to live … and for what? … so that you can see a young innocent boy suffer from cancer and die, and there is nothing you can do about it? Just let it all out partner; tonight is YOUR NIGHT!"

The words all made perfect sense – why would anyone else care what happened to him? If he cracked up, he would just end up on a table like so many others he had seen before – then it would be *their* job to put *him* back together. Well, wouldn't THAT be poetic justice?!

The rain continued to pound, as the defiant duo made its way south. After awhile, Evan began to ignore the quiet, haunting refrain of Addy's voice, until it finally went away. He heard thunder, saw the twinkling of lights in the distance, and felt galvanized. He threw his head back in laughter, as he rounded a sharp bend. Suddenly, he saw a massive flash of bright light … then, everything went black.

The next thing he remembered was a feeling of being suspended in a vast sea of nothingness. He found himself motionless, as if his body was completely frozen. Yet, he felt no heat and no cold. There was no way he could move any of his limbs, though he tried, and there was nothing but darkness around him. He started to panic, but then he felt a cool breeze on the top of his head, and he began to hear voices.

"Wait just a minute" he thought. "I have traveled this road before."

Chapter 5: "Easy Does It"

Evan's eyes flew open. The first thing he saw was Margaret, sitting over him, watching him with tenderness and compassion. Walter stood off to the side, leaning against a wall, with his arms crossed. Margaret reached a gentle hand down, as if to whisk away strands of hair from the younger man's face. Surprisingly, Evan caught her by the wrist. His cold gaze met hers and he asked, very deliberately, through closed teeth, "Where - is - Addy?"

She felt the anger in his grip. Pulling away, Margaret quickly got up and left. Walter continued to lean against the wall; he didn't move a muscle. He just continued to study Evan, with a slight scowl on his face.

"What are you looking at, old man?" Evan challenged.

"Must've been some dream!" Walter responded.

Evan suddenly remembered the events that led up to his sleep. "You all drugged me!" he said in a booming voice.

"We had to", Walter said. "It was the only way we could ensure that you would have an uninterrupted sleep. It was necessary for you to be able to see everything that happened to you just before you arrived here. Whatever it was that you saw, you will see again when you sleep … tonight, tomorrow night, the night after that …until you have seen the dream seven times."

The younger man started to sit up and Walter rushed over to assist him.

"Easy does it", he cautioned. "You might want to just lie back and listen to me for a few minutes. You're starting to come around, but there are a few things you must know before we start out. There is quite a bit we have to do today, and I need to prepare you for it."

Fighting through his anger, Evan complied. If nothing else, the old man had shot square with him, up until now. His patience was unlike anything Evan could possibly imagine. Still, he secretly harbored a thought as to how he might be able to provoke his host into a fit of rage that might match his own.

Walter slowly made his way over to where his guest was lying, and began to speak. He chose his words very carefully:

"I know that you are angry, but I can't tell you why. You are going to have to sort that out for yourself. But now that you are here, I can tell you that it will eventually go away; and you will be reunited with Addy, when the time is right. Now, I have something important to show you. Once you have seen it, you will need to be off on your way - to go to work."

As soon as he said the word *work*, Evan instantly thought of Dr. P and he anxiously thought about his return to the harvesting field. He didn't know exactly what the work might entail, but he did kind of look forward to being able to see Mark again. Wait a minute! Mark? Mark Pickford? Of course! Mark was not only a doctor, but also his colleague. All the thoughts of the work that lay ahead of him started to weave through the creases of Evan's brain.

"What are you thinking about?" asked Walter. He noticed the distant stare pasted on Evan's face. "Perhaps something from your dream is starting to make sense?"

"Sort of" Evan responded. "I'm sorry I got angry with both of you just now. I don't know why I'm so angry. Well, actually, I think I do. I was angry pretty much through my entire dream ... and it involved the death of my son."

"Don't tell me anymore!" Walter said, as he turned away and showed the younger man the palm of his hand, motioning for him to stop. "You will be able to tell your story in a few days, to a group of elders. You have to experience the dream at least four or five more times before you can do that, however. All the details have to be crystallized; then they can be made into a story. But you have to focus on all the events, because you must be able to recite your dream before every remnant of it vanishes away."

"That reminds me" started Evan. "You were telling a story yesterday to the children on the hill about a man with the same name as me. What was it all about? Was it about me?"

"You weren't paying attention, huh?" challenged the elder. "It was probably the anger and thoughts of Addy that clouded your ability to focus."

"Exactly!" Evan rifled back. "How could you possibly have known that?"

"Okay, this may be a little hard to absorb all at once, but I'm just going to tell you this directly" Walter confided.

"Here in *Backstep*, the oldest people know most everything, but they lose a little bit of that knowledge with each passing *dip*. A dip is when the sun sets at the end of each day. That's when the knowledge of everything beyond seven days is erased from your memory forever. Only people who are eighty years of age or older possess a collective memory beyond seven days."

The older man continued. "I am quickly approaching my eightieth year, in reverse, as a matter of fact. Anyway, between now and the next dip, many of the things about *Backstep* will become more and more clear to you, and you will understand why you are here and what your immediate purpose is. You will also understand and become comfortable with the fact that Margaret and I will be here with you until you no longer exist."

Walter made his way to a cupboard, and pulled out some bread and something that looked like dark jam, perhaps blackberry or black cherry.

"We need to eat a little something before we go", he said, as he motioned for Evan to take a plate. "Once we finish eating, I'm going to take you to the place where the journey eventually ends … for all of us. I have to tell you as many things as I can, while I can still remember everything. Every time the sun dips, we all lose a little bit of our own stored knowledge – it's as if we become a little less intelligent every day. But every time there is a dip, we each become a little less polluted … we are that much closer to perfection."

"But that's impossible" Evan argued. "Don't you know that nothing is perfect? That's one of the FIRST things that we learn on earth!"

"Ah, but this is a different life. Here, in *Backstep*, you arrive as an imperfect being, then you work your way backward toward perfection. In the world where I came from, the only perfect thing in the world was the birth of a child. Now, we all get to experience that perfection again – and it awaits us all, in time."

The two men quickly finished their small meal. Then, they began to make their way back toward the hill, where they had first joined together. As they walked along, Walter pointed out things: children playing and people talking … lots of positive interaction, everywhere.

The sky was a bright blue once again, and the sun warmed their skin as they walked. When they got closer to the hill, Evan saw another old man (dressed similar to Walter), leaning against a rock. He was telling a story to a group of children, as well as to a few adults. This was almost exactly the same scene he remembered from the day before. At first, he didn't pay close attention. But then, he began to vaguely recognize some of the others, though he didn't know how that could be possible.

When they got closer to the hill, they broke off onto another path. This one curved around a large mountain, and they made their way at an ever-quickening pace. There was a sense of urgency in the way Walter walked, and Evan marveled at how a man of over eighty years of age could be so spry. As they walked, he suddenly became aware of others who had joined them on the walk: men and women, some about his own age (he suspected), and others who were slightly younger. Most everyone carried a small, tightly-wrapped bundle. The people didn't say much as they walked, but he noticed that a few of them were shedding tears. Walter slowed their pace a little, as if to keep a little bit of a distance between the two of them and those carrying bundles. Everyone appeared to be headed for the same place.

A near-blinding light shone around the rim of the mountain. Walter pointed it out with his walking staff.

"That," he indicated, "is the *Light of Pureforth*. It represents the achievement of perfection. All these little bundles you see are little ones being carried to the light. When they are placed in the special basket, they are transported to everlasting peace. They can only be carried away when they are perfect. Today is the day that they have all reached that last dip in their own respective journeys."

"But how do the people carrying the bundles know when the little ones are ready?" Evan wondered.

"Good question. Do you see that they are all wrapped tightly? That is because they are shining as brightly as the light that we are approaching. When the light shines off the little ones, the time has come to bring them to this place. They are so bright, in fact, that they are impossible to look at directly. The light is the ever-constant guide."

"So are these people like the parents of the little ones?" Evan asked.

"In a previous world, yes. The same joy that these people experienced in another life, in another place, they get to be a witness to once more. The only difference is that in THIS place, there are no childbirths. So, once the little one has been sent off to everlasting peace, there is no lasting grief. That's just one of the things that makes this place different."

"So this is kind of like death? That must mean that the harvest field is more akin to birth, in a way ... except that there are no biological parents, as you said. That's certainly a good thing for the mother!" he mused.

Walter cracked a smile when he said this, and nodded his head. "Yes, that's one thing in particular that Margaret enjoys about this place!"

Gradually, all the travelers came to the entrance of a tremendous cave, guarded by a majestic stone door. One by one, the groups carrying their precious bundles entered and then disappeared into the bright light. After a few moments, they re-emerged; this time, no longer carrying anything. Evan noticed that there was no apparent grief on the faces of those he gazed into; rather, it was almost as if the people had received some sort of relief – like a duty fulfilled, or a wonderful and arduous task accomplished.

"I can only imagine how they feel" sighed Walter. "One day I will, though ... the day I carry you here, in my arms – along with Margaret, of course. You see, this is how we each make our exit ... as helpless little infants ... perfection achieved!"

"I'm beginning to understand a little better now," Evan rationalized. "By living life backwards, we each undo the bad things we have done, erase painful feelings and memories, recapture the things that we lost at one time or another (in another time and place) and work our way back to total and complete innocence – it makes sense in a way ... but I still have many, many questions."

"So do I, but I'll answer what I can."

"What I would *really* like to know is this: Will I know everything I know now as I re-trace the steps of my life?"

Walter rubbed his chin with an old, wrinkled hand: "Everything your mind retrieves between now and the next dip of the sun will stay with you for seven more. After that, you will lose a little bit of your collective knowledge – day by day. But that only happens once you drop below eighty years of age. As I said before, those people eighty and older know virtually everything –"

"Wait a minute!" Evan interrupted. "Is that why we saw all those old people on the hillsides, talking to the children? They are kind of like the teachers of this society, right?"

"Close enough", nodded Walter. "Just like me, their gift to society is the ability to recount stories –stories of people and things that have already happened ... only their audience doesn't know that they are actually the protagonists of these stories. I will have the capacity to do this for only a short while beyond this day. There are others who are already losing their abilities to teach; for some, today is the last day of teaching – and they know it. My time is just around the corner."

"It must be tough to give up something that seems to bring so much joy to others" Evan concluded.

"You might think so" the old man winked. "However, once they are done with this valuable service, they stop telling stories and they start living the rest of their lives. That's when life really begins; after all, you're only old once!"

Chapter 6: A Brief Stop Along The Way

As they left the cave that contained the *Light of Pureforth*, Walter and Evan walked alongside many people who were bubbling with joy. They couldn't help but become caught up in the infectious light-heartedness of those who surrounded them. However, Evan was deeply confused and conflicted. He could not seem to get past the haunting memories of his dream and of losing his son in a previous life. And where was Addy?

A couple of times, he had tried to share the contents of his dream with Walter, and each time the old man had denied him the privilege. This just made Evan even angrier. "I thought he was supposed to help me deal with my anger and help me get better!" he secretly seethed. "Certainly, this place can't be *everything* he has said it is, or I would be a much happier person!" They walked along the path, away from the mountain – away from the light ... away from perfection.

Soon, they happened across another hillside. An old man was holding court with a group of children, and several adults. The man's name was Isaac. Although he was greatly aged, he seemed much more supple and vibrant than some of the other teachers Evan had observed along the way.

"Let's stop here, just for a few minutes", pleaded Walter. "I would like to hear my good friend Isaac, one last time."

It suddenly occurred to Evan that Isaac must be one of the teachers that Walter had mentioned – those who would experience their last day of teaching and then move into the "living" phase of their journey. The two men settled onto the cool grass. This time, Evan was able to shove aside his anger and keep his wanderlust at bay, in order to pay close attention to what the man was going to say. He believed that there must be some help hidden somewhere within the message he was about to hear.

"Good day, little ones", the old man began. Evan chuckled at this. After all, it *was* a good day. It would certainly not be the last good day. Isaac paused for a moment before he began, as he was flooded with the realization that this was to be his last time performing as a story-teller. He chose his words deliberately:

"I am going to tell you a story", he started out slowly. "There was an old woman who all the people in the village loved. She was kind; she planted beautiful flowers, cooked wonderful meals and always surrounded herself with friends. There was only one problem: sometimes she would suddenly become sad and cry. No one around her knew why – it seemed as if one minute she was very happy and then, without warning, her mind would drift off and she would appear lonely and despondent. Whenever someone would ask her the question as to why she was feeling so low, she would always force a little smile, brush away her tears and say, 'Oh, it's something that will eventually go away. Every dip is one dip closer to true happiness'".

Evan cast a sudden glance toward Walter. "I think I know just how she feels" he whispered. "Since I've been here, I've felt this nagging anger; and yet, somehow I know it's going to go away – I just don't when."

"Things are starting to become clearer to you now" Walter nodded. "Listen on."

Isaac continued with his story. "This woman had a hidden secret that she didn't really want to share with anyone; and there were two main reasons why she never would let anyone else in on it."

"Why?! Why?!" the children collectively screamed out. They were rapt with attention, and their curious little minds grappled with myriad possibilities.

"Well, people start out separated from ones they really care about. But after awhile, those people always seem to come back. For some, it takes longer; for others, only a brief instant. But the people you know, the ones you care about, are always there with you until the very end. That's the wonderful thing about this place. If you look around you, you will see lots of happy people – this is all you need to ever concern yourself with."

Isaac talked on and on, in flowery tones. Everyone was drawn in by his speech ... mesmerized. He then concluded with these words: "Be happy ... run and play ... be as free as a child. Perfection, my dear ones, lies in the hearts of little children."

Everyone started to clap fiercely, as some of the adults in attendance nodded their heads, smiling with approval. Some of the adults dabbed at their eyes, truly touched by the sentiment. One, an older attractive lady, sat fairly close by. When Isaac had finished, she slowly walked up to him and grasped him by the arm.

"How do you feel?" she asked.

"I feel both relieved and a little saddened", Isaac confided. "It's nice to be able to have all this knowledge and to be able to share stories of collected wisdom. But I'm ready now to spend more time with you."

"I have been looking forward to this also", she said. "Now, if you will allow me the privilege, Mr. Templeton, I would like to properly escort you to your final meeting at the Council of Dreams."

"I would be delighted, my dear" he countered, as he offered his arm properly. She gently clutched him just behind the elbow and the two walked off. Evan noticed that they both seemed to have a little bit of a spring in their steps.

"Council of Dreams? What in the world is that all about?" Evan wondered aloud.

"Oh, you will come to find out, up close and personal, after another few nights of grappling with that dream of yours," Walter snickered, although he was being serious.

The two men got up from where they had been sitting and listening to the last story that Isaac would ever tell. They watched the children disperse, as well as all the people wearing purple cloaks (Evan no longer had his). They all ambled in different directions, some to be caught up in various games of tag, hide-and-go-seek, and blind seekers. Others just grabbed the hands of the older people who accompanied them.

Evan saw the adults pairing up with much older people, just as he had noticed before. "Everything here seems to have a very familiar pattern" he observed.

The two men continued to walk together. As they did, they became silent for a prolonged period. Their silence took a back seat to the gaiety and frivolity that surrounded them – the happy children, the cool breeze, the warm sunshine, and the sight of everyone with someone else. No one was alone. Witnessing all this, he halted abruptly, grabbing Walter by the arm. Seemingly frozen in time, Evan blurted out a random thought that had smacked him from out of nowhere.

"Do you know who Isaac was talking about in that story?" he asked. Walter stopped suddenly and his smile turned serious and contemplative.

"Yes … and so do you."

Chapter 7: Return to the Field

As the men continued their walk, Evan was becoming more and more comfortable with his surroundings. It was odd to him how life went on here – people had jobs, though many seemed vastly different from those he remembered in his dream. People were farming, cattle were grazing, goods were being transported – that part was all normal to him. As he looked up into the sky again, he saw lots of blue and an occasional soft, friendly cloud. It was the same scene that he remembered from the day before. He casually contemplated if there could ever be a gloomy, rainy day in this sort of place.

"If everything goes in reverse order, how does the whole eating thing work?" he wondered aloud.

"Yes, that always seems to be a point of confusion for the new arrivals", rationalized the older man.

"Let me try to explain it in a concise way, that won't further tax your already-overwhelmed mental capacity. You see, there is another harvesting field, just on the other side of town. From that field, we gather all of the food that we need until the sun dips in the eastern sky. We don't store any food at all – we simply take what we need ... nothing is wasted, and there is no such thing as a surplus. If we eat beef, that's what we get. Farmers are paid for nurturing the tender plants and the animals, until they reach their own respective points of perfection – the point at which they are consumed. It seems strange at first, but then – like everything else – it becomes just a normal part of the accepted routine."

"But if things work in reverse, shouldn't we be throwing up our own food?" asked Evan. "It seems to me that if everything happened backwards, we would be taking food out of our mouths and putting it back on the plate!"

"From your point of logic, as a newcomer, that's understandable. Some of the acts from the previous world are similar. Many of the things we do, the meals that we eat, even the feelings that we have … all occur as forward steps. At the end of each day, it is as if we have taken one large step forward. When the sun dips and we go to sleep, we are then greeted with the same dream that we keep having over and over. Upon waking, it is as if we have taken two large steps backward. We can recall the events of everything that has happened to us seven days into the future, which is actually our past in this particular life. Everything beyond the seven days of our collective memories is whisked away into oblivion … the good memories as well as the bad memories."

Evan scratched his head. "I suppose that's why I didn't see any photographs in your house. There's no use preserving things that you don't even recall happening to you."

"That's absolutely right", Walter agreed. "Actually, photographs used to exist in this land. But once people started to lose the use for them and their value fell to nothing, that particular technology eventually went away. The reason I know this is because it has only happened since the time I was harvested. Sometimes I tell the story about photographs to the children. It's one of my favorites – for more than one reason."

Walter seemed as if he was about ready to launch into revealing another secret or two, but he suddenly checked himself. "Back to your question: we only take what we need, we eat everything we take – there is no waste, there is no starvation. Also, since there are no waste products, nothing leaves the body! Another interesting thing that contradicts the "conventional wisdom" that you brought with you to *Backstep* is that sometimes you feel really full and miserable before you begin eating, and you often feel hungry and empty after you have completed your meal. The more you consume during the meal, the greater the effect before the meal even starts."

"You know, I do seem to recall that I only started to feel hungry AFTER we ate this morning", said Evan. "So that part is in keeping with the way things seem to work in this backwards world."

"After another day or two, you won't even notice it anymore. It just becomes another part of your routine. You begin to live backwards pretty effortlessly."

The whole time they were talking, the two men continued to move in the direction of the harvesting field (the one that harvested humans).

Evan already felt like he knew the way perfectly, even though he had only traveled it once before. As they approached, he noticed groups of people – families, or so it appeared – coming and going. No one was alone. This was a recurring theme; and yet, he wondered to himself: if this is true, and people are reunited with their loved ones – why was Addy with him for only just a brief moment or two? This particular thought started to make him angry again. Walter sensed this, and he began to stew over what words he might offer to the younger man, to ease his mind and prepare him for the work that awaited him.

"Okay, we're nearly at the field", he said with a voice of eager anticipation. "I am to leave you with Mark, your friend and colleague. Your job is that of a harvester. The two of you will be working together, to pull people out of the ground so that each can begin living his or her own life here in *Backstep*. It's a really wonderful job and you should feel privileged to have it."

"I don't see what's so great about it!" Evan griped. "It's just pulling people up out of the ground – and it doesn't really sound like much of a job to me!"

Walter stared at the younger man, fighting off his disbelief at this flippant attitude. "It's so much more than that" he said. "You will be providing a service that will bring groups of people together and will set the foundation for entire lives. It's so much more than just 'pulling people up out of the ground', as you so caustically put it. Mark will show you everything that you need to know and the duties you must be able to perform. Hopefully, by the time the sun dips again, you will be ready to be more independent in your work. Now, do you think you will be able to find your way back to my home when your work is done today?"

"Yes, I feel certain that I can. Check that; I *know* so. Suddenly, I feel as if the way has been firmly imprinted in my brain. It's amazing how some of the things I say and that I know just seem to kind of pop out, with no reasoning or explanation … they just happen. Now, before you leave me here, I wonder if you could just answer two more simple questions for me."

Walter stopped and fixed his sharpest glance at Evan. He did not want to have to answer too many questions, but he felt like he owed him a little bit of latitude, since he was still considered a newcomer to this place. "Okay, I'll try to answer your two questions" he said. "But that's all, for now".

"Fair enough. I just want to know if my anger will go away and if I will see Addy again – both before the next dip of the sun."

Walter fumbled for words. He wanted to tell everything he knew – and yet, there was only so much information that he could truly reveal … for now. His words came out very cautiously, with a certain degree of concern.

"I don't know about your anger", he began. "It seems that there is a lot more of it than there was before, so I don't know if it's going to go away that quickly. But as for Addy …" he paused for what seemed like an excruciating period of time … "I believe you may see her, but only from a distance. I cannot tell you why; I can only hope that you trust me when I tell you that you will be seeing a lot more of her very, very soon. I don't know the exact details, but I have a very strong feeling about it. That's all I can offer you, for now."

Evan was extremely irritated. "All right, I suppose I'll go do my crummy job and jerk complete strangers out of the ground. It'll be good to have something to be able to take out my frustrations on!"

"That's not a very good attitude for your first day on the job", warned Walter. "Perhaps you should just watch, listen, and learn, rather than offering up a few more shards of your own boiling commentary. Mark has been looking forward to your arrival … he really needs you."

"Yeah sure, he needs some guy whose just been harvested, to help him harvest others – it makes total sense to me!" Evan's sharp sarcasm was not a source of comfort to Walter, by any stretch of the imagination. The old man started to wonder if leaving him here was, even remotely, a good idea; yet, he knew that it was something that had to be done – there was no avoiding it.

As they got within a few steps of where Dr. P was waiting, Walter turned away to head back to his favorite hillside, where his own work would begin until the next dip of the sun. Before departing, he made one final plea toward the angry man who was beginning his first day on the job:

"Please just try and give it your best, most patient and caring effort" he implored.

Evan watched for a few moments as Walter walked by himself toward the hillside. It was the first time he recalled seeing anyone walking alone, and just for a brief moment he felt sorry for the emptiness he knew that the old man probably felt. He was immediately snapped back into reality with a bold slap on the back and a hearty, spirited greeting from Dr. P.

"Well, well, your first day on the job!" Mark exclaimed. "I have been extremely busy of late, and I am so glad that you have finally arrived to help. For the last few days, I have eagerly anticipated your arrival ... and now the time has come!"

Evan was a little uncertain, but he did his best to shake off his indecision and do as he was told. "Okay Mark, tell me about this field and exactly what I'm supposed to do."

"You may think pulling people out of the ground is an easy task, but there's much more to it than that. It's not so much *what* you do, but rather *how* you do it. Basically, strangers will come up to you and identify themselves. As soon as they tell you who they are, you will lead them to a specific place in the field where you simply wait. I still haven't figured out exactly how I know where to go – some mysterious higher force or power just leads me there."

"Anyway, once you get to the spot, you start to hear rumbling and you feel the earth move beneath your feet. Then, a head starts to push up out of the ground. This is the really important part: the initial shock of seeing a loved one for the first time can be very overwhelming for some. That's why you must act quickly, pulling the body out of the ground, usually with some assistance, and then carefully covering it with a large purple wrap. Secure the wrap around the person to keep him/her warm, as well as to protect the individual's modesty. Then, stay with the person until one of the orderlies takes charge. At that point, you give way to the younger subordinates, then move on to the next new arrival. There are several harvesters, but now that you're here, our work just got a whole lot easier!"

"I think I understand, although it still seems like a pretty easy job. By the way, I just noticed that the purple robe I had on yesterday is no longer around.

"So you noticed", his friend acknowledged. "We cleaned it up really well; now, it can be used by someone else. You shall never wear a purple cloak ever again."

Evan looked over to the stack of neatly arranged purple garments. There were slight variances in shades and sizes, but they were all of a distinct, deep rich violet hue.

"Purple is the color worn by those who have just arrived. You wore yours from the time you were harvested until you first slept. While you were sleeping, it was taken away, laundered, and brought back here. It will be re-used ... nothing here is wasted."

"I see", said Evan. "I did notice that all the people wearing that color were being led around, and that some of the colors were very bright, while others were somewhat faded."

"Exactly! ... here in *Backstep*, we maximize the use of every single resource; not necessarily because we have to, but because we are all making a conscious effort to bring ourselves that much closer to simplicity and perfection. It is all part of the process."

Suddenly, Evan's temper began to steep once again. "Well, if things around here are so perfect, then answer me this: how come my loved one – Addy – abandoned me, shortly after my arrival? I would think that she would have been the one to take charge of me and take me home yesterday!"

"Okay, that's a fair question. I promise you that once we are done with our work today, I will enlighten you a little more. It's a lot to absorb in such a short period of time. Just watch me for the first few harvests. Before you know it, you'll be doing it on your own ... in expert fashion, I might add."

Mark grabbed his colleague by the arm and the two of them started walking toward a small gathering of people at the south edge of the field. On the way, the doctor grabbed a clean, finely pressed purple wrap and tucked it under his arm. They didn't say a word as they made their way over to the small group. Everyone appeared nervous and a little scared. Evan began to have some of the same feelings himself.

"Hi, I'm Mark", he said to them. "But you can all call me Dr. P. Now, who is it you are here to claim?"

A gray-haired woman, leaning on the arm of a much younger man, looked up into Mark's face and said, "I'm here to claim Craig Whitehouse."

A thought immediately shot into Evan's brain. "Craig!" he thought. "That is the name of my son." As he began to vaguely recall some of the details of his dream from the previous night, he just shook his head. How could anything so terrible happen to such a young boy? He felt the anger rise, but it gave way to a second thought that popped into his mind, as he looked into the delicate eyes of the woman. "This must be his wife ... and it appears that they will be together for a very long time. I wonder how long she has been missing him."

"My name is Sarah. I have been waiting so long for Craig's return!"

Dr. P took the old lady by the arm and guided her over toward the middle of the field.

He stopped, and held up his hand, as if to silence everyone around him. But then, Evan started to notice a strange movement in Mark's fingers. It appeared that he was testing the air, for a sign of some kind. It seemed very strange and rather mystical. He looked at Sarah and said, "This is the spot. Now, turn around, close your eyes and begin humming your favorite song. Ask the others to join in with you."

Sarah did as she was told and began humming a sweet tune; the others fixed upon it, and their voices took up the words that went with it. The music seemed to put Mark in an almost trance-like state. He blew on his fingers to warm them, and then watched the surface of the ground, for movement. Evan felt a trembling sensation near his left foot. Looking down, he saw the top of a head beginning to protrude from the ground.

"Clearing, over here!" Mark shouted. He placed his hand on top of Sarah's and said:

"I'm going to ask that you keep facing the other way. Please keep singing, because Craig can hear you. Once he's covered, you can look at him."

Sarah and the others did as they were told. Mark then turned around and guided the man out of the ground in a smooth yet brisk fashion, then quickly covered him with the purple cloth. He tucked the edges under and around the man, both to protect his dignity and to keep him warm. After he had cleaned off the face and hands, he helped Sarah to kneel down beside the old man. She put a wrinkled hand near his face, and began stroking it. Craig slowly opened his eyes. He was dazed and confused – it was a look of near desperation. Evan remembered that look – oh, how he remembered that look!

"Craig, Craig … Craig." She leaned down and began whispering gently into his ear, and he fell asleep. She then looked up at Mark and asked, "When can I take him home?"

Dr. P smiled and gave Sarah a re-assuring pat on the shoulder. "Not to worry", he said. "Once Craig is ready, one of the staff members will take him to a hillside, where he will begin his journey. When the time is right, we will bring him to you. You just go home, for now."

"Oh, thank you doctor!" a relieved Sarah offered back. She kissed Mark on the cheek, then grabbed the arm of the younger man who had accompanied her, so that he could lead her back to her home. Just as she was walking away, the doctor called for a young lady (perhaps only eighteen or nineteen), to come over. He whispered some instructions into her ear and pointed toward one of the nearby hillsides. She nodded her head in understanding, then knelt down beside Craig, to maintain watch as he slept.

Evan was curious. "What did you just tell her?" As he asked the question, Mark was already rushing toward another group of people, now assembling on the far side of the field. Not sure of whether or not Mark had heard his question, he asked it again, as he rushed to catch up.

"I simply gave her some instructions about where to take Craig and who to hand him over to, once he is ready. My work with that group is done … it's time to move on."

Evan was beginning to process things. He realized that Mark met up with people, led them to a spot, instructed them prior to the harvest, harvested the body and briefly prepared it, oversaw the family reunion, gave some instructions to both the family and a member of the harvesting staff, and then moved on to the next family. It seemed routine, and yet very significant.

"C'mon, hurry up! We've got work to do!" Mark now had a pronounced urgency to his movements, and he seemed energized after another successful harvest.

"Do these harvests ever fail?" Evan asked.

Mark wheeled around, faced him and smiled. "Never!" he said, with a gleam in his eyes. "This is an absolutely wonderful job, because there is NEVER a failure."

As the two men moved from family to family, Evan noticed that Mark seemed to be gaining strength, energy and speed with every new case. He was becoming less tired throughout the day, which made sense, considering that he was now living in a backwards world.

The process seemed the same; the only variation was in the direct interaction that he had with the various assemblies of people who came to claim their loved ones. In the deep recesses of his mind, Evan recalled the term 'bedside manner'; a term that came with him from the previous world. He seemed to remember that Mark had always shown a kind and patient bedside manner. Evan was beginning to realize that there were some similarities between being a doctor here and being one in the world that he came from. He didn't know it then, but very soon that belief would be blown apart.

Chapter 8: "It's What You Make Of It"

Before the dip of the sun, Evan finally got a chance to handle one of the cases on his own. As much as he wanted to trust the new doctor, Mark felt much better about closely monitoring him for his first solo harvest. Evan made his way over to a group of three people. Politely and professionally, he asked them to identify themselves and asked them to say the person's name who they were claiming.

As soon as he was told the information, he heard a strange buzzing in his ears. A voice in his head said the words, "Follow me", and he repeated these words out loud. When the words first came out, he was momentarily stunned, but he was quick to regroup and take it all in stride. As he turned toward the center of the field, an unseen force moved him to a specific spot. To the side, Mark smiled because he knew that Evan was succumbing to the power that the doctors possessed as they worked in the fields.

"Only the doctors who ask the questions are given the answers", the voice continued. "Now is your time, Evan. This is your purpose ... what you have been called upon to do. You have a talent; you have both power and influence. But be careful, this can be a gift or it can be a curse – it's what you make of it."

Evan was able to shake off the penetrating words enough to be able to perform all the necessary tasks to complete this particular harvest. With purple cloak now in hand, he positioned the people around him to his right. He instructed them to hum, which they did. He told them to turn around at just the right time. He held out his hands, felt the tingling in his fingertips, and finally his eyes fixated on a spot where he detected some movement.

A small head began to push up out of the ground; but before he had a chance to free the body from its subterranean cocoon, he was hit with a sudden realization – one that he had not paid attention to before, because he was so focused on the order in which he had to perform his duties. The thing he had failed to give notice to was the fact that these people were all much younger than all the others he and Mark had worked with throughout their case load that day.

As he pulled the body out, he gazed into the face of a young boy – perhaps only about eleven or twelve. The body looked like it had been through some kind of torture, and Evan was glad that the others were facing away so that they couldn't bear witness.

The doctor carefully laid out the body, covered it with the purple sheeting, tucked it properly around the body (just as he had observed Dr. P do several times before), and then turned to the group of people gathered to his right. Just before he opened his mouth to speak, the mysterious voice came back and said, very firmly: "Do not say anything to anyone about the state of the body … the purple cloak is transforming it into an acceptable form, so that this young man may begin his journey here in *Backstep*."

A young man! Evan was hit with the realization that this boy was about the same age as the son he had lost; his dream flooded in to haunt him once again. He fought back his rage just enough to be able to place a hand on the woman's shoulder, and give her the last set of instructions. He was angry about the fact that such an innocent-looking creature could have endured such punishment. Also, he was enraged about the fact that THIS family would get to see the return of a son – and yet here he was, with no Craig and no Addy. It simply wasn't fair! He curtly gave the instructions to the woman to go home and await the young man's arrival. Just as he was ready to leave them, the woman turned, grabbed Evan by the wrist, and reached up to give him a delicate kiss on the cheek.

"I dream about you every night", she said. "You did all you could, and I know that. But all good things come to those who DO good things, and YOU DO GOOD THINGS!"

"Thh-thank you", Evan feebly responded. He was absolutely dumbfounded. His anger went away as quickly as the air out of a popped balloon. For a moment, he stared at the family as they left, as he continued to stand over the body. Just behind him, Mark cleared his throat in order to gain Evan's attention.

"Flirting with the patrons, I see", he quipped. "Well, you're not quite done yet, Mr. Popularity", he teased.

"Oh, right!" Evan summoned one of the available staff members over, to give the final set of instructions, before moving on to the next case. When the orderly arrived, he looked toward Mark with momentary panic – he didn't know what instructions to give! Realizing this, Mark held up his hand, with his palm facing toward his friend and colleague. He then took a deep breath, and spoke.

"Breathe deeply", he said. "Close your eyes. Let 'the spirit' take over".

Evan remembered the voice from before and did as he was told. It buzzed in his ears and tickled his brain; it told him where the boy was to be taken and who he was to be delivered to. He began to further advise his assistant about proper care and patience toward the new arrival, and the girl (now kneeling beside the boy) interrupted him by shooting him a cold look and saying, rather defiantly: "I know what I'm doing ... I've been doing this a LOT longer than you have!"

As Mark tried to stifle his chuckling, Evan scooped his humility off the ground and made his way to the east end of the field, where another group of people waited quietly. After many harvests, he noticed that he felt stronger and more refreshed with each and every case he completed. His energy levels were up, and there was plenty of work yet to be done. Groups of people were arriving now with greater regularity. The two doctors walked together for a few more steps, before Mark started to peel off in another direction.

"Business is picking up", he said. "I believe you're ready to do it all on your own now. Just be calm, be patient, and listen to 'the voice'". He started to talk louder, as he pulled away in the other direction. "I'm needed over here, but I'll catch up with you later."

The two doctors worked the rest of their separate case loads. They brought joy into so many lives that day, and there were about as many purple-cloaked figures walking around *Backstep* as anyone could ever recall on any particular day. Finally, as the sun began to dip, people stopped coming. Evan had already finished with his last case, and he waited for Mark to finish his. When the veteran doctor had seen the last assistant off with the last new arrival, the fields were empty and quiet.

"Isn't another shift going to come relieve us, or something?" Evan questioned. "Won't there be more harvests throughout the night?

"No, harvests don't happen at night ... only during the day. That's just the way it is. Now, it's time for us to go. I told Walter that I would take you back to his house. Besides, there are a few more things I need to tell you."

"Good, because I have a few more questions."

"I am sure you do. Well, just understand that there is only so much that I know. I can recall events from the past seven days, and I can tell you, very vividly, some of the details of the dream that I have every night. Other than that, I can tell you more about the job, and about what we do at the end of each day."

As the two men made their way along the path toward Walter's house, Evan paused. "There's really not much in the way of machinery here", he observed.

"Oh, there used to be; or at least, that's how I understand it. This place used to be a real decadent society, so much into technology that the people were always rushing around and confused. As time progressed, the people gradually became more simplistic in their values. Large buildings started to be de-constructed, clothing became a lot more basic and functional, and people started entertaining themselves more by reading and writing and telling stories."

Evan thought for a moment. "I noticed that Walter's house was very shabby and didn't have very much in it. Is he a poor man?"

"Perhaps poor, in terms of possessions; but he doesn't need many things right now … that comes later."

"Oh, I see … or, at least, I think I see. People start out with not much, then they have people give them things as they enter the prime of their lives, then they basically lose all of those possessions as they become small children, at which point they really don't care about possessions at all … is that about the size of it?"

Mark stopped him cold. "Hold on there, friend. You are trying way too hard to overanalyze this life and this place. It doesn't work the same way for everyone. People arrive at *Backstep* at different ages, and their lives play out on individual stages. You can't figure it out and you don't know what's going to happen. What you DO know is that your life will end when you are perfect, and you are working toward that right now. Your individual journey will take longer than it does for some, and will be much shorter than for others … like Walter, for instance."

After thinking he had just begun to figure out this new world, Evan was now plummeting into as much confusion as when he had first arrived. Little fragments of memory were coming into his ever-filling mind, and he was still battling with the feelings of losing Craig and being abandoned by Addy. He did his best to shake it off and focus on the present.

"So where are we going now?" he asked.

"I'm taking you to Walter's house … you have a dream to catch. It's very important that you get lots of sleep and concentrate on the details of your dream. Many of the things that you see and hear will remove some of your confusion, before the next day arrives. After you have had the dream for the seventh and final time, you will make your appearance at the Council of Dreams."

"I've heard that term before", Evan countered. "Walter mentioned it; or maybe it was Isaac …I don't know; I forget". As he said this, he began to hit the side of his head with the heel of his hand.

"Don't hit your head like that … it just got pulled up out of the ground!" Mark joked.

"Yeah, but it was a pretty good day today." Evan cast a smile in his friend's direction.

"It's about time I saw that smile of yours!" he remarked. "I can tell you have really been battling some personal demons, and I know a lot of that comes from your dream – whatever your dream may be. Just keep focusing on the details - it is very important that you do that. It will be a big help when you make your appearance before the Council."

"So, what is this 'Council of Dreams'?"

"Well, it's basically a gathering of all the elders … the storytellers … you know, the teachers … people like Walter. Once they are assembled, people are brought in who have been in *Backstep* for only seven days. These are people who have had the same dream every night, since their arrival. Before they start losing some of their collective memory, each person gives a detailed account of his/her dream to the members of the Council.

In turn, the Council takes the images and weaves each one into a story. These stories can then be told to the children, once they are cleaned up a little, of course. They spend the rest of their time preparing other stories. Some of things they tell about are based upon their own observations; others have been handed down by the elders who preceded them. It's been such a long time that I have absolutely no recollection of how my meeting with the Council went. But it's pretty much the same for everybody."

"So I am to appear at the Council of Dreams after I have this horrible dream a few more times?"

"That's the way it works."

"Well, I can tell you this: some of the contents of that dream are still haunting me now, and are making me very mad. You probably saw some of that anger come out earlier, and I apologize for that. It wasn't intentional, and it wasn't aimed at you."

"I know that."

"It's just that – in my dream – I lost my son. I got really angry and then I just stormed out into the night, hopped on a motorcycle, and ---"

"STOP! I don't want to hear anymore! Actually, I'm not *supposed* to hear anymore. Look, we're almost at Walter's house. You should go inside and let both Walter and Margaret get you prepared for sleep. From what you started to tell me, it sounds like you're in for a bumpy ride. Now, go get some rest."

Mark placed a reassuring hand on Evan's shoulder as he turned to walk away. He was very glad that he hadn't been asked any more questions about Addy, because he knew how painful this time of separation must be. He felt an extreme sense of relief that he had staved off what could have been a potentially disastrous situation.

Evan entered the home of Walter and Margaret. They both were a lot more relaxed and happy than we had left earlier that day. A table was already prepared, with a much bigger meal than what he had eaten before. "I don't really feel like I can eat much of anything. Actually, I feel full!"

"That's good" offered Margaret. "That's exactly the way you are supposed to feel before a good meal." Evan let out a little bit of a laugh; it was going to take a little more time to adjust to this new way of living. This time, Walter and Margaret both joined him at the table.

"We usually say a little prayer before we start", Margaret indicated as she nodded her head toward Walter. "Would you do the honors, dear?"

Walter closed his eyes and held his hands upward, making somewhat of a production out of his every movement. "We now would like to ask blessings upon the food that will now empty us of a little more of our evil and knowledge. Thank you for the steps we take toward perfection ... Pureforth!"

"Pureforth!" echoed Margaret. She then began passing the food around. Evan had thought that maybe some other word would end the blessing, but he wasn't sure exactly what word (or words) to have expected.

"So tell me about your first day at the harvesting fields", Walter pried.

After thinking about where he might begin, Evan started to recount how he felt when he first arrived at the place of the harvesting, and the sight of Walter walking away all by himself. He told of the families that he and Mark had helped to reunite, and the confusion of this strange power that seemed to take over when he was in the field.

Margaret listened intently, somewhat in awe of the newfound power that the younger man was quickly acquiring. Even Walter began to feel a little small, in the presence of his guest. But it was not an envious feeling; rather, one of pride.

When they finished their meal and everything had been cleaned up, Margaret brought over a cup of hot tea. "Now this is the same tea that I made for you last time", she said. "It will make you sleep soundly. You might want to sit on the edge of the bed, before you start drinking it; you remember what happened before?"

"So this time, you're actually *telling* me that you're going to drug me!" Evan blurted out. He intended for it to be more of a light-hearted comment, but it came out a little caustic and rough. Walter seemed to get the joke, but Margaret appeared a little hurt and defensive.

The younger man apologized to her, and she smiled back. He dutifully went over to the bed and accepted the cup. Very soon, his eyelids became heavy, and he was slowly transported back to Presbyterian Memorial Hospital – to another life.

Mark didn't have far to travel for his evening meal. He had grown accustomed to these dinners, and it never got old to him. Well, how could it? He was going backwards! Things simply didn't grow old; they got younger and happier. As far as he could remember, he had attended seven of these dinners. He didn't recall exactly how many he had been to, but it didn't really matter.

As he opened the door to the welcoming hall, he was greeted by several people. Everyone there was someone he recognized – people he had actually harvested, their families, and other people who were close to him – family and friends, alike.

"Hey look everyone, it's Doctor P!" All sidebar conversations ceased, as he made his way through the masses, toward the head table. He stopped along the way, to chat with several people and to receive the thanks and accolades of many others.

As one of the guests of honor, Mark Pickford had grown very accustomed to the fanfare. He tried to be humble, but it was difficult. He moved behind the table, and settled in toward the center. Keeping his place for him was his partner, Terri. She pulled the chair out so that he could move in, and as the crowd continued to applaud and yell his praises, she leaned up and softly spoke into Mark's ear.

"Are you still mad at me? How did everything go today?"

"Actually, it went very well. He held up even better than I thought he would." He leaned in, kissed her delicately on the lips and apologized for the disagreement they had earlier.

"Does he know yet?"

"No. On a couple of occasions, I was afraid it might slip out. Serendipity must have truly been on my side. He's a smart one, though; he picks up on a lot of things very quickly."

He continued to smile and wave at the crowd. After a few more moments of people paying him homage, everyone sat down for the feast. Mark looked at all the food and didn't know how it could possibly be eaten, but he knew that it would.

As he placed his hands on top of the table, he wasn't sure that he could even eat one single bite. He had begun to feel full from the time that he and Evan had begun their trek back to Walter's house.

An elderly man walked in front of the head table, directly in front of the honored doctor, and banged a glass to get the crowd's attention.

"And now…" he began, "we pay our respects and give our thanks to a hard-working, kind and caring group of harvesters. We give our thanks to you …"

He turned to face Mark and the other eleven doctors and their families. Then, as he raised his glass of wine, he exclaimed: "To the Light of Pureforth!"

"The Light of Pureforth!" the crowd echoed, in unison. This was the only formality of the entire proceeding; the rest was simply food, conversation and the enjoyment of living – as a community. After this dip of the sun, none of these people would remember what any of these professionals had done for them. With the next fall of blackness, they would go through the same thing with another throng of people – same thing, different faces.

Mark looked to his right. Seated at the table with him were Doctor David Dials and his partner, Erin, along with two young girls. Just beyond them sat David's harvesting teammate, Justin Majors. Gretchen, his partner, sat next to him, along with a very young boy. David and Justin had worked together for as long as they could both remember, and their families were seemingly joined at the hip.

Glancing back to his left, he looked back into the face of his partner of many years, who was seated next to him. On the other side of her sat a fifteen year-old boy, who had only recently started to join them at the dinners. Mark was glad to have his family with him to share these moments – he knew that eventually they would not be holding these in his honor, but for someone else as well.

Further down the table sat another doctor, Jake Krueger, who had been with him a long time. Jake's partner, Lucille, was there too. They added a lot to these dinners. This particular day had been an odd one for Jake, because he was not a doctor anymore, but merely an orderly for David and Justin. His days as a doctor were over; but he would still have six more dinners to be treated like one. He didn't care though, because he was young and very much in love. Lately, he had been thinking less and less about work and more and more about freedom and playing around. That's just how it was when you grew younger.

As much as he would miss their company, Mark had known that they would be moving on, so Jake's impending absence wasn't as much of a blow to him. What he was really happy about was the thought of having those same chairs filled by his new professional partner, and his family. Evan could not possibly know how much Mark was anticipating his presence, and how eager he was to invite him into this wonderful nightly experience.

Although he felt bad about not mentioning anything about it to Evan earlier in the day, he knew the reasons why he had to maintain his silence. It would be great to share all of this with the one who bore the same name as the fifteen year-old sitting next to Terri.

He had been doing his best to properly prepare Addy for this part of the transition. She was a very delicate flower; she always had been – for as long as he could remember, although he could only remember seven days past. One of Mark's secrets that he could not tell Evan was that he dreamed about her every night … because Addy was not only Evan's partner, but she also happened to be Mark's younger sister!

Chapter 9: More Than Just A Visit

When Evan finally woke up, he felt better, but a lot more troubled than after he had experienced the dream the first time. Overriding the anger was a sense of hurt – he was deeply distressed by the pain he must have caused Addy and the members of the hospital staff that he had walked out on. Had he actually killed himself? It appeared so. That's probably why she had such a hard time facing everyone around her when he first arrived at *Backstep*, he surmised. He made a vow to himself that he would try and make things right – perhaps he could issue a heartfelt apology to Addy and make things better. Then he thought,

"What good is an apology going to do? It can't change anything" … and besides, he was beginning to understand that, here, time actually erases things.

Breakfast with Walter and Margaret was very quiet, almost somber. It was as if each person had plunged into a deep period of inner-reflection, knowing what had to be done on that particular day, partially overshadowed by certain memories. The three people were all at different stages of knowledge: Walter had a much larger collective memory; Margaret had a vivid recollection of the past seven days, but no more. Evan, after only two full days, was still gathering bits of his mind, grappling with the details of his dream, and recalling his initial experiences in this new place.

Walter finally broke the silence. "You seemed to rest a lot more peacefully last night", he indicated. "You didn't thrash around nearly as much. That's good – some people have a very tortuous sleep, when confronted with their dreams. Perhaps your dream isn't really that awful."

"That's what you think!" Evan countered, almost apologetically. "There were some pretty horrible things I saw, and there are several wrongs that need to be righted. I'm just not sure if I can, and if so, exactly *how* I can."

"Realization is the first step", said Walter. Margaret sat close by and offered not a word; she simply nodded her head and added a re-assuring smile. The three family members continued their breakfast, and then dutifully cleaned up afterwards.

"So, you're off to the harvesting fields?" prodded the old storyteller.

"Yes. I'm pretty familiar with the routine now. Still, I get this funny feeling that this day is going to be much different – maybe even special."

"You just never know", Walter said with a smile.

Margaret began to gather a few things: a light jacket, a scarf, and a large pushcart.

"It's time for me to go to the field market", she indicated. "I've got to go there early so I can get the best pick of what's available."

"Anything you pick will be fine", said Walter. "I'm already getting hungry, just thinking about it." He had already wrapped his cloak around him, preparing to make the journey to his familiar hillside. After last night's meeting of the Council, he was anxious to try out several new stories on the children.

Evan was the first to leave. As he walked away, Margaret leaned in to Walter and whispered, "Is this the day that *it* happens?"

"Yes" he whispered. "Meet me there shortly after the second meal." They watched together as the young harvester headed toward the field and his job, having no idea what was in store for him.

In another part of town, a middle-aged woman was looking in a mirror, dabbing her eyes. Night after night, she had been haunted by visions of a man who left his previous world in a terrible way. When he had stormed out of the hospital, he had destroyed not only himself, but her as well. After he died, she eventually re-married, but could never shake the images of him or their son, Craig. Now, finally, it was all coming back. When the next dip came, she would attempt to bring Evan home at last.

The field was just as it had been left the day before. David and Justin had already arrived, and they were working together on the first new arrival: it was an elderly woman; so old, in fact, that everyone naturally assumed that she would be telling stories for quite some time – and they would be right! Evan strode across the uneven ground, noticing that he had gotten there a little ahead of Mark, but he knew that his partner would be arriving soon. As he continued to think and process bits of information that were deluging his brain, there seemed to be something strangely familiar about Mark – something he hadn't noticed yesterday; but for some reason, he still couldn't make sense of it all.

"Oh well, no matter", he thought. "I hope it will be as busy as it was yesterday. If it is, maybe I'll be able to take my mind off the horrible images of last night."

A family had assembled near the north edge of the field. One of the members of the group looked a lot like a certain young man he had harvested the day before. As he made his way over, he could not seem to shake the vision of Craig from mind – not the man he had harvested, but the boy that he had seen ripped away from him during the night, in his dream. He started to feel anger and a sense of loss. Bravely, he fought these feelings off, as he approached the group that anxiously awaited.

Able to focus on his duties, he performed all the necessary tasks that his specialty required. Just like yesterday, he became more alive and energized with each passing hour.

Evan could almost remember a time, in a previous life, when he would labor on and on until he was bone-tired; but this was totally different. This was much more enjoyable!

Once Mark got to the field, all the other doctors were already hard at work. Sometimes, the case loads seemed to mount all at once; at other times, they were spaced out just enough for the men to be able to engage in idle chatter. The orderlies didn't get this particular privilege – they had to rush around, gather harvesting supplies, make sure that enough clean purple sheets were readily-available and, above all else, carefully tend to the new arrivals. As David and Justin watched Jake Krueger rush around the field, very disheveled, they wondered how he had ever been a doctor. They were also somewhat amazed that Evan had not recognized any of them by now. In time, though, they knew that he would.

As the day wore on, the sun rose directly overhead. The air warmed, but it didn't get very hot – it never seemed to get either too hot or too cold in this place … everything was pretty temperate, which was in keeping with the mood of the entire society. Evan was feeling very good as he walked over to another couple, at the west edge of the field.

"Hi, I'm Evan", he cheerfully greeted them. The man and woman looked up, with sadness in their eyes.

"We've come to claim Richard Foster", the woman said. Her tone sucked all the joy right out of the young doctor's soul. Usually, people were *happy* to rekindle with a loved one. Something was terribly wrong here!

He guided them to a spot in the field, and the harvest was completed in routine fashion. This time, however, as Evan went through the now-familiar rituals, he felt a kind of impending doom and evil lurking about him. At first, he attributed it to his dream; but as he looked deeper into the eyes of the Fosters, he wondered if it had more to do with Richard and the kind of life he led before.

Richard was lying stretched out on the ground, safely and warmly tucked amid the purple cloth. As he was being tended to, the couple stood motionless nearby. No one reached down to him, no words were spoken – there was just a hollow, empty silence. The woman buried her face in her hands and bitterly wept, as they began to move away. Evan felt his heart begin to break for the family, and he wondered what terrible secrets might be hidden in this life.

He reached down and placed his hands on the tops of Richard's shoulders, just as Mark had done to him before. Gazing down into the strange man's face, he said these words: "I don't know you, but I *believe* in you." The man continued to sleep, but a smile gently spread across his dry, cracked lips. Evan would see this man again; he just didn't know it yet.

Across the way, Evan looked up and thought he saw a very familiar face – the face of … no! It couldn't be … but, sure enough, it looked very much like Addy! He brushed away the notion, at first, because he knew that she really wouldn't have any purpose here.

When he looked up again, he saw Walter and Margaret and a couple of other people he didn't recognize. They were gathering around at the other end of the field. He wanted to break away and find out what was going on, but he was right in the middle of another case. David had already arrived to meet the group, so he had taken over. He saw the lips move – the verbal exchange between David and Addy. She looked over in Evan's direction, but when their eyes met, she simply looked down toward the ground. Just as he thought his heart might break, something occurred to him. At that very moment, all the faces and names of the doctors became known to him, and he truly knew what was happening. He worked feverishly to finish up with the person he was working on so that he could join the others.

After what seemed like an eternity, Mark came over to where Evan was working. He put his arm around his friend.

"*Now* do you know who I am?"

Tears welled in Evan's eyes as he answered the question. He had recognized Mark at various stages the day before, but his mind had continued to cloud, causing his memories to become distorted – before then, all he could really focus on was anger, his dream and – Addy.

"Yes, I do. Can you take me to her now?" Dr. P smiled, nodded his head and began leading his colleague toward one edge of the field. The others were standing in a semi-circle, looking down at the body of a twelve-year old boy, shrouded in purple. Stroking his face, knelt down beside him, was the boy's mother – Addy!

Evan came over and placed a hand on her shoulder. She looked up and their eyes met. Slowly she got up and threw her arms around him. They tightly clasped each other and she began to sob, uncontrollably. He said nothing; he just continued to hold her. Evan then repeated the same words to Addy that she had said to him previously:

"I am right here with you." He had been so absorbed with Addy that he had almost forgotten about Craig. He looked down at the tender face and the gaunt body of the sick boy. "Things will get better … I promise", he whispered. Lost beneath her tears, Addy was able to cough up a reply: "Oh, my dear, they already have!" As she said this, she looked over Evan's shoulder, caught the eye of her brother, and beamed a smile of relief and gratitude. Evan continued to hold Addy, as he looked down upon the face of the young boy.

"Okay, I hate to break things up", Mark unceremoniously announced. He looked at Evan. "You and I have more work to do, my friend." He then looked over at Addy and said: "You go back home and I'll bring Evan to you, once we're done here. That'll give you some time to get Craig settled."

Addy reached over and gave her brother a huge hug. Mark was elated. This was the first time he had seen his sister truly smile with happiness in a long time. It looked like the family was whole once again. Walter came over and shook hands with Evan.

"Congratulations", he said. "I guess you probably realize that you won't be coming back to our house tonight."

"Yes, I suspected as much", Evan nodded.

As Addy walked away, she kept looking back over her shoulder at her two loves, both of whom had been taken away from her much too soon. They had both been in her dreams every night, compounding her misery and suffering. Now, she knew that when she woke up the next day, those dreams would give way to the reality that life was truly good again, and that the perfection she had always been told about and that she had ached for was now finally beginning to unfold. She was now ready for the next step of her journey!

Evan wanted to stay with his son as long as he could, but Mark convinced him that it would be better if David continued to work with the young man, until he was ready to go to one of the hillsides. The doctors continued to work with their case loads, until the sun started to dip. When the last of the harvested souls had departed that day, Mark and Evan left the field, but began walking in a different direction – one that Evan was not yet familiar with.

"I haven't been this way before", Evan admitted. "Are we going where I *think* we're going?"

"Boy, I can't get anything past you", Mark said as he slapped his colleague on the back. Soon, they rounded a sharp bend and came to a rolling valley. Midway down the slope, there was a cottage with smoke coming out of the chimney. It was a quaint little place; it didn't look too cheery, but Evan thought he understood why that might be the case.

Mark looked on as they worked their way down the hill, to the door of the small abode. Having finished just his second day on the job (and his first full one), the doctor reached for the doorknob, then froze. He turned around and looked back at Mark, and asked,

"Should I knock first?"

"What are you talking about?!" shouted Mark. "It's your own house!"

Before opening the door, he heard voices inside. He recognized Addy's; but there were two others – both seemed to be those of young boys. Evan took a deep breath, turned the knob, and went into the house. As he did, Mark just smiled to himself and walked away. He had somewhere else to be and, if he wasn't careful, he would be late – again!

Chapter 10: Two More Mouths To Feed

It had been quite some time since Addy had to worry about additional places at her table for meals. She didn't know exactly how long, because her memory could only go back seven days. It was always a treat when Alex came around – he paid periodic visits, as a nephew often does. As he was growing younger, those visits were becoming more and more frequent. Now, he had even more of a reason, with the arrival of his cousin. Addy knew that since Craig's father had returned, it might confuse him to meet a family member who had part of his own last name as a first name.

Addy also wondered how she was going to break the news to Evan – what would be the best way to tell him one of the two big secrets that she had kept hidden from him throughout his former life? She and Mark had been planning to tell him many times that the woman he had fallen in love with, married, and had a son with was actually his own sister. For reasons Addy had always wanted to keep private, they had lived separate lives and kept the truth hidden. Addy and Mark saw each other almost every day, in the other world, but the families had been kept strangely apart. This was one of the "wrongs" that Addy had so very much wanted to fix, and now she was finally going to get her chance. The only dilemma now was finding the right words.

She re-focused her attention on the two cousins; primarily, on Craig. He had only been in *Backstep* for the better part of a day, but already he had become comfortable with exercising his contagious sense of humor. Even though his body was ravaged by the effects of cancer, he didn't complain and he battled through the weakness that his body displayed.

"Too bad you don't have the same last name as me. You could be Alex Alexander!"

"Just call me A.P! Do you think you can handle that, Craig-head?"

The two boys laughed as they continued the little name-calling game that they had made up on the fly. They had almost forgotten about the fact that Alex, the older and stronger of the two, had practically carried Craig on his back the whole way to the house. For the next few days, Craig would need to be carried almost everywhere – but the promise was there that he would get better, stronger, more and more perfect with each passing day – and they both seemed to know that.

Everyone looked up when Evan came walking through the door. Addy commenced with the introductions, and to carefully reveal a long-hidden secret. Evan had to become familiar with a partner, a son, and (soon) a nephew he never knew he had. All of this seemed like a tall order for a person who had only been in this new land for such a short time. Evan let his eyes scan the room – he supposed that the surroundings would become familiar soon enough. Looking over toward Addy, he noticed that the smile on her face was constant, which certainly made him happy. There were several burning questions in his mind; but they could all wait. Right now, he simply wanted to drink in the wondrous details of what had every appearance of being a happy life – even despite Craig's cancer.

"Alex, may I put down another plate for you, for dinner? I can certainly divide out all the food; it's no trouble".

"No, that's alright; I need to be getting back. I still have a couple of errands to run for my dad before dinner."

"See you tomorrow, 'Sick-o'", he fired toward the younger boy.

"I can't wait, you big ape!" Craig cast a big, toothy grin as he sprawled out across the bed. They both burst into laughter, as Alex headed out the door.

Alex didn't like to lie, but he had just told one. The "errand" he was running *was* his dinner, although he felt like he was doing this as more of a personal favor for the rest of the family. Dinner, for him, was always a big spectacle now – and he really didn't like it. But he had been told that, very soon, more family members would be attending those dinners, and he wouldn't feel so alone. At this point, he had been sworn not to say anything to anyone, especially to Craig. He had almost let it slip out to Craig on the way back from the hillside, but he had caught himself just in time. Craig would not be able to attend the banquets right away, but he would in due time.

Evan went over to Addy and offered to help her get the meal ready. She instantly turned around and gave him another crushing hug, very similar to the one that she had given him in the field, upon his arrival. However, this time there were no tears.

"I have missed you so much", she said. "All this time I have been sad, but it's very difficult when you don't know how or when it will go away. Eventually though, you know that it will. These past two days, I have received two very special gifts. My bad dreams can no longer touch me."

"What kind of dreams do you have, Addy?" Evan wanted to know as much as he could about his partner. He felt like he owed her so much, although time was now helping him slowly undo all the hurts and ills that had accumulated from his previous life. He feared he was largely to blame for the nightmarish visions she had; he pondered how many nights she had been forced to submit to them, in helpless terror and grief.

Addy looked into Evan's gray eyes. "I don't want to talk about my dreams", she said. "Just know that you and Craig are both in my dreams every night. Some of the things that pass through my mind are not the prettiest pictures in the world. But with each passing day (and night), I am getting younger and younger; I feel more alive and I have much more energy.

With the arrival of you two (she cast a glance over at her son), I have more around here than just two more mouths to feed." Not wanting to press the issue, Evan chose not to pry any further as to what twisted images must pass through that pretty head every time the sun dipped down behind the massive mountain in the east. He was gaining more vitality, more courage, and more knowledge. Bit by bit, the names and the faces of those around him – those who loved him – were flooding into his stream of consciousness. He began to wonder if all this would complicate matters when he fell asleep again and confronted the demons that awaited him.

"So, they tell me I have to appear at this place called 'The Council of Dreams' after I have this dream five more times", he said. "Is there anything special I need to know before I make my appearance in front of all the elders?" Evan was truly curious about what he might say, and how he might describe the things that he saw. He was pretty sure that he could do it already, down to the last horrific, ghastly detail. But he also knew that, perhaps, with several more opportunities to confront his past, he might be able to make better sense of the events, and that, just maybe, it would better serve him as he continued his trip backwards.

For now, the couple was just happy to be together. Neither one could imagine a greater feeling of joy. However, they both wished better things for Craig. They knew the promise of good health was on the way, but they didn't know exactly how many of Craig's remaining years would be strong and happy ones … only time would tell. Though they didn't say anything about it to one another, both Addy and Evan thought on their own about what it might be like on the day when they both would carry Craig, tightly bundled, to the place where he would be taken off to absolute perfection – for the rest of eternity. They had both been shown the place; they both knew of its significance. But still, they didn't see it as an important place in their lives here; and they really didn't want to.

Alex had lost track of time. He repeated both of his new nicknames to himself as he walked: "A.P … Ape … A.P … Ape …" As he tossed the names back and forth, he wondered: "Which one is really me? Which is the one that truly reflects my identity? Am I important enough to simply be known by my initials, or am I really an ape, like Craig said?"

He shook his head; he had been talking to himself out loud like some kind of crazy person. There was only one thing on his mind now, as he began to pick up the pace of his steps. He did have another "errand" to run, but it had nothing to do with his father. What he wanted more than anything, right now, was to see the smile, the green eyes, and the dark auburn hair of the girl that he was absolutely smitten with – her name was Lisa. He began to whistle as he skipped along, with his hands in his pockets. To think – he had just gained a cousin, everyone in his family seemed much happier, he was young, strong and good-looking (or at least he thought so) and he was in love with a girl. How could life possibly be any better?

After Alex's departure, Addy and Evan walked over to where Craig was reclining. He seemed pretty tired, but it did not show on his face; only the rest of his sick body showed the effects of what he brought into this world with him.

"Is this my spot?" he asked. Evan battled back a tear and he reached down and patted the boy on the head. "Yes, indeed", he lovingly responded. "You are with us for the rest of your life, buster."

"Bust who?" the young lad said, with an infectious smile. His comment caught Evan quite off guard; meanwhile, Addy threw her hand over her mouth and tried her best to suppress the sudden laughter that erupted from within. How was it possible that a boy in such a ravaged physical state could manage to keep the good humor sustained? It didn't seem possible. "But since you two can't be my mom and dad, I guess you'll just have to be my 'star' and my 'hero'. Can you figure out which one is which?"

"Well, there can only be one 'star' in *this* household", Addy played along, as she placed her hands on her hips and threw her head back in a very exaggerated manner, trying her best to be like a famous actress.

Evan looked at her and was truly enamored. He instantly agreed that Addy was, in fact, the 'star'. Craig nodded with approval. "You guys are pretty smart for old people", he winked. "Hey 'hero', when the sun comes back out, can you take me to a place where there are other kids like me? For some reason, I think I may be able to help them."

"I would love to, but I have to go to work. Maybe your mom – uh – your 'star' can take you."

"I know just where to go", Addy beamed. "Although, once we get there, I have a strong feeling that I'm not going to be the 'star' anymore." She smiled at Craig and then she looked over at her loving partner. Perhaps the sickness that was here in this room was helping everyone in more ways than they all knew. Many times she had heard stories about kids recovering from cancer – she had heard those stories from parents and from little children. They were told over and over by the elders, so they must be true. She began to feel that this particular young man was going to have a significant impact - not just on her, but on all the inhabitants of *Backstep*.

The three people gathered around the table for their first meal together. None of them ate very much, and they all caught themselves staring at each other. As they continued to partake, Addy knew that she was going to have to administer the drug to two people, before sleep. They would sleep soundly through the night as they battled their own personal apparitions. Addy also believed there was a very good chance that she would probably wake up a few times during the night. This time, when her eyes opened, however, she would see a full house and she would know that things were actually getting better, not worse. She thought about taking some of the drug herself, but she only had twelve doses – seven for Craig, and five more for Evan.

Once the dinner was finished and everything was cleared away, both parents gathered around Craig to give him instructions about drinking the tea and about having to face up to the same dream he had before coming into this world. They warned him that he might see some bad things, but that he shouldn't be worried or fearful.

"Are you both kidding me?" he scoffed. "If it's the same dream we're talking about, it's the most wonderful dream I could possibly think of having. Let me at it!"

Both parents were stunned. Was this another attempt at a joke? Were these things being said by a child who simply didn't want his parents to worry or fret? Or perhaps his dream truly was a pleasurable experience. They both wondered what awaited the young man once his eyes were closed. They sat with him and watched him drink his tea. He then stretched out his arms, let out a big yawn, laid back and instantly went into a deep sleep. They noticed that he had a peaceful smile on his face. His parents had no way of knowing this of each other, but they had each seen this same look on his face in their own dreams. How could such pain produce such peace?

Evan was next. He dutifully drank his tea, and before he could fall asleep he looked into Addy's eyes and said, "I'm sorry for everything. I'll do everything I possibly can to make things right for both you and Craig." He felt a deep pang of guilt and remorse as his eyes began to glaze over. Sleep hit him like a freight train. Whether he actually heard the words or not, Addy didn't know; but she offered them up anyway, as she kissed him on the forehead:

"There is nothing to forgive. Yesterday, one of my special gifts was delivered to me. Today, I have received another. I will live out the rest of my life in happiness."

Chapter 11: Behold, Our Champion

The first stream of light came through the north window. As it filtered in, the dust particles dazzled in golden flecks and danced all the way down. Craig was sleeping peacefully. His body was slightly contorted, but he still had a smile on his face. Evan, asleep just across from his son, was smiling too. His rest had been more fitful; he tossed and turned, and had every appearance of being much more anguished in his dreams. Addy had been up for awhile; as she watched them sleep, she wondered what she might find, given the chance to dive inside their heads.

Craig was the first to wake up. He slowly stretched, yawned, and then searched-out Addy. He blinked his eyes a couple of times and then said, "Wow! What a dream! I hope I have the same dream again tonight." Of course, Addy had guessed that he would, but she said nothing. She wondered what spectacular things he might have seen, and debated about whether he could have possibly been faking it, just to make his mother feel better, or whether these dreams were as magical as he indicated they were. But when she really thought about it, she recalled that the smile never seemed to leave his face. She began to realize that Craig was one truly amazing kid, and not just because he was her son. Before the next dip of the sun, she would come to see this young man in an entirely new light.

Very soon, the other pair of eyes opened. Evan's sleep had once again been a ghastly trip that he couldn't bear to re-live; however, he remembered Walter's words and wanted to be able to recount as many details as he could when he appeared before the Council. Some of the images were still very clear in his mind, though he dared not speak of them to the other members of his family. This was his own private war, and he was determined to win it.

When Addy noticed that Evan was finally awake, she rushed over and gave him a light peck on the cheek. "There you are", she said.

"Yep, there's my hero …getting ready to go start a few more lives today!" chortled the ailing boy.

The bluntness of Craig's words stunned Evan. He had not really paused to think about the nature of his work, but the meaning of what Craig said rang true. Indeed, Evan was getting ready to get a few more lives started … started on the road to perfection. He felt proud, honored and very lucky. Somehow though, as he looked over at the sick boy lying on the bed, he didn't imagine himself to be nearly as lucky as Craig.

"How can someone be so sick and yet be so happy?" he pondered. "He is truly a miracle and he is bound to have some extraordinary purpose here. I just wish I knew what it was, and that I could help him reach it in some way." He continued to think these thoughts – all through breakfast and as he hastily got ready for his trip to the harvesting field.

"Are you two going to be okay by yourselves today?" he asked.

Addy and Craig looked at each other and both burst into laughter.

"Well, that about answers my question! Take care, my dears." He saluted them and headed off to work. He was sure that today would be the best day of his life. He tried to imagine how any of his remaining days could possibly be bad ones.

After the man of the house had taken his leave, Addy adopted a bit more of a serious tone as she began to carry on a conversation with Craig.

"I need to explain to you why your father never knew about my side of the family. Mark and I were going to tell him; we really were. Things, however, kept getting in the way … the right moment never seemed to present itself … and then, it was too late."

"Hush, my shining star", replied Craig. "Whatever your reasons may have been before, they don't matter now. The important thing is that our family is all together and that we are happy. Now we have to turn our attention toward making *other* people happy – because I detect a lot of sadness around us."

Addy was in awe of the magnitude of the young man's wisdom and rationale. It was rare that someone could arrive here and have that kind of attitude, so early. The fact that his body was ravaged with disease just made it that much more amazing.

"So, handsome, what are the two of us going to do today?" she beamed.

"I thought we'd go down to the Children's Hospital; you know, to the cancer wing. There are a lot of really sick kids there, and I feel like I need to go cheer them up …give them some hope. Don't ask me why; I just feel like I need to be there."

"Somehow, I figured that's where you wanted to go. You don't have to say any more; that's exactly where we'll go. After that, I have a big surprise for you, for dinner tonight."

"A surprise?"

"Yes; although I suppose I could tell you now, if you really want to know!"

Craig studied her for a moment with his eyes, trying to decide whether or not to call her bluff. Then, he cast a reassuring smile and said, "I'll leave that up to you."

"Okay, I'm going to tell you, because I find it hard to keep secrets anymore. Tonight, you and I are going over to Alex's house for dinner."

"What about dad?"

"Well, your dad and my brother have a special dinner to attend. Terri, who I told you about, is cooking up a wonderful meal for the four of us – just moms and sons!"

"I hope the guys have fun, but they are really going to miss out, aren't they?"

"I don't know, it really doesn't seem like any of us miss out on very much!"

Mother and son got ready and Addy got the customized wheelchair fixed up, to push Craig toward the hospital. She didn't mind doing it, because she knew that his condition would improve and that he would soon no longer need it. She didn't know exactly how long that might be, but she wasn't worrying too much.

It was another lovely day. There were wisps of white streaming across an endless blue sky. Warm sun and a light breeze greeted them as they made their way. Craig talked periodically, but he mostly wanted to drink in the environment and point things out to his mom – things he had never seen before.

Addy engaged him in dialogue as best she could, but she found herself going back to last night's dream. Something had happened; the terrible images she had seen night after night, since the time she had met with the Council of Dreams, had gone away. She could vaguely remember going on a picnic with her two men. Everyone was happy and Craig was running around, just as happy and healthy as she could ever imagine.

"How could this be?" she wondered. "If these are supposed to be visions of things past, I must have lost track of something, somewhere. Dreams can be so confusing!"

Craig started humming a tune; Addy joined in. As the pair neared the hospital entrance, they were both happy. The song was one that Craig had heard in his dream; it was the same one that Addy had been singing when Evan was pulled up out of the ground.

"How does he know this song?" she puzzled.

Life in the cancer wing of the hospital was just as they both suspected it would be. There were lots of sick kids everywhere. Most were simply too tired to do anything and laid around all day. Some complained about feeling worse than the day before, and a few actually felt a little better. What Craig detected, more than anything else, was that these children didn't have any hope – they had all been *told* they would get better, but not many actually believed it. He had to do something to make them see – to understand – that life was a pleasant journey and not a single moment of it should be wasted, even if one happened to be sick.

Craig thought for a moment, then whispered something into Addy's ear. She looked at him as if to question him, at first; then she nodded her head. With his assistance, he slowly raised up out of the chair.

"Look at me everybody!" he yelled. "I'm a jellyfish!" With that, he let go of the hand rests and went sprawling onto the floor. He started convulsing violently in front of his wheelchair; but he wasn't in pain. As he was thrashing around on the floor, he was laughing – almost uncontrollably. "It's easy", he yelled. "Just think of something else – then BE it!"

Craig had drawn a crowd. A young girl, about his own age, who was lying in a bed nearby, rose forward and announced to anyone who would hear:

"I'm a seal!" She then began clapping her hands, drawing them way out past her sides first. As she did, Steffy Konrad started making the loud, comical barking noises of a seal. She stopped, momentarily, and looked toward Craig, who was still on the floor.

"Hey, this IS fun!" she exclaimed.

Before anyone in the hospital knew what was happening, kids were jumping off beds, rolling around on the floor, making strange noises and faces at each other, and having a great time. Some of the adults, who looked on, smiled in acknowledgement; a few of them had dreams at night of a young man who would come to the hospital and bring hope to all the sick kids in the ward – THEIR kids. Now, they knew that the prophecies were coming true and they could finally attach a name and a face to the spirit of hope and the promise of recovery – the name was Craig Alexander.

The day just seemed to fly past. No one had ever seen such joy and happiness in all their lives – not even among those who were never sick. Craig tried to make his way around to as many new friends as he could, but he was in so much demand that it was a virtually impossible task to get around to everyone. In time, he came to a bed where a very sick boy was lying.

"Do you know how long you've been here?" Craig asked.

"As long as I can remember", came the feeble response. "But I'd like you to do something for me, if you can, before you leave."

"You name it, and I'll do my best", Craig promised.

"Help me up. I need a couple of adults to brace me as I stand, right up on top of this bed. I've got something to say to all these people."

Doing as he was told, Craig summoned a couple of others and they helped Bart Thompson to his feet. Standing in nothing but his hospital gown and sock feet, supported by an adult on either side, Bart fought the wobbling of his legs and raised his arms toward the ceiling. In his best announcer voice, he sounded off:

"Ladies and gentlemen! Welcome to Children's Hospital! Today, you have witnessed an epic battle between the forces of good and the evil darkness of cancer. For many days and many years, we have held these battles and the mighty cancer has come out on top ... but TODAY (he raised his voice and both arms again as he said the word), we have in our midst a secret weapon against the roiling despair and the sapping of strength ... we have someone in our midst who will show us the way to truth, to light and to good health ... I give you – Craig Alexander! Behold, our champion!"

Wild cries of "hurrah!" and deafening applause sounded through the wing of the hospital. As she clapped, Addy felt tears of pride streaming down her face. A couple of kids rushed over and grabbed one of Craig's arms and lifted it into the air. Others patted him on the back, thanked him, or simply cheered his name. This was certainly not the way Addy had expected the day to turn out. But it was unmistakable now what Craig's purpose in *Backstep* happened to be. The fact that it had come about so quickly was a little overwhelming, but everything about Craig seemed to happen freely and naturally.

As they made their way back home, neither Addy nor Craig were the least bit tired. The day's events had bolstered their strength and their confidence. After all this, they were getting ready to add even more enjoyment to their day, by having dinner with a group of relatives. This would give Craig a chance to meet new people and would provide another opportunity for him to clown around with his cousin, A.P. Who knew what kind of trouble they might be able to stir up next?

Walking along, Addy began to ask a few questions of her son.

"I'm just curious" she wondered. "What kinds of things do you see in your dream?"

"Well, you know, I'm not really supposed to tell you" he cautioned.

"One of the elders explained to me that I have to tell my dream before the Council after a few more nights of the vision."

"That's correct" Addy responded. So far, everything seemed to be following a pretty normal pattern; Craig seemed to be just like everyone else.

"But I'm going to have to really study this dream" he continued. "In the middle of everything going on, some voice keeps telling me that the dream I have will keep repeating every night until I am actually carried into the bright light of Pureforth."

"You mean, your dream won't go away after the seventh night?"

"That's what the voice keeps telling me … but it's only been one night. Maybe I didn't hear it clearly. I hope the voice is right though, because – what an AWESOME dream!"

Addy wanted to know more, but she was almost afraid to venture any further into Craig's other world. A couple of times she made thinly-veiled attempts to get him to explain some of the details that swirled around his brain during the night, but he casually brushed her off. Finally, she asked him directly:

"What was your dream about, honey?"

"It's really too difficult for me to explain to you."

"Do you think I wouldn't understand?"

"The truth is, mom, I don't really understand it all yet. I really need to have it a couple of more times, at least. Regardless of what happens tonight or what the voice tells me, I know exactly who I need to sit down and have a talk with."

"Who, your father?"

"No … HIS father. I need to talk to Walter."

Chapter 12: Hello To Youth

He was only beginning his fourth day in the land of *Backstep*, and it was his third one as a harvester. However, on this day, Evan had an unusual degree of energy; he couldn't imagine that things could get any better – especially after having recovered from his horrible dream the night before. He remembered that, upon waking up, his very first vision was of the angelic, peaceful face of his son on the other side of the room. All the things that he hoped to be able to reverse now seemed possible – seemed within his reach. There were things he wanted to say – to Walter, to Addy … and to Craig. But right now, there was work to be done.

Mark had arrived early and was waiting for his colleague. Evan had done an excellent job the day before, and Mark was confident that today would be a repeat performance. He hoped that the day would be exceptionally busy; it would cushion the blow of the potentially devastating news he planned to lay on the newcomer at the opportune moment.

No sooner had they exchanged pleasantries when the time came for them to make their respective ways to opposite ends of the field – Evan to the north, and Mark to the south. They greeted the families in the customary way, conducted their business, and sent people on, filled with relief that another family member had arrived to live a life toward perfection. As Evan finished his first delivery; Mark couldn't help but notice that his friend was quite good – in fact, the best he had ever seen!

Before either of them knew it, they had worked their way through the entire morning caseload and they were able to take a brief break for lunch. They knew the time to eat had arrived when they both began to feel full stomachs – that was always the signal.

Evan didn't want to spend a lot of time away from his work. He felt more alive, more vivacious, with each passing minute. Still, he paused long enough to share a bite and a word or two with his faithful co-worker.

"You are good ... REALLY good!" Mark admitted.

"Thanks. You know, the funny thing is that I have been working all day nonstop, and it feels like I've been doing this job my whole life."

"If you look at it in technical terms, you almost have" responded Mark.

"I guess you're right. I've been in this field every day since I've been here!"

Mark tried to nonchalantly bridge into what he really wanted to say to his friend, but his penchant for subtlety was somewhat lacking. "I have a confession to make" he blurted out. "Look in my eyes. Do you notice anything?"

Evan took another bite of his sandwich and gazed into Mark's eyes as if he were truly looking for something; however, he seemed confused. "What am I looking for?" he finally asked. "Is there something in there that I need to take out?"

"No! Seriously, though - Do these eyes remind you of anyone else's?" Mark asked. "Study them for just a moment."

"Well, since I don't personally know a whole lot of people, I can only guess that you're referring to a member of my family."

"Good .. go on."

"So - you have the same eye color as Walter, they're shaped a little like Addy's and they have a glimmer kind of like I have seen when I look into Craig's eyes. What exactly are you driving at? Are you some sort of mutant?"

Mark paused for a moment. This dialogue was not going at all like he had hoped. He simply wanted to get it over with. "Look, this is not easy for me to say. Since before you arrived, I have been waiting to unload a confession to you. We are, in a way, related. You see, Addy is ... my sister."

Evan stared at him for a moment, appearing rather nonplussed.

"Now before you get angry, I can explain. In the old life, both Addy and I wanted to tell you, but time and circumstances just got away from us. Then, it was too late." His partner interrupted him before he could go any further. "Look, in my brief time here, I have come to realize that not much of the logic from the other world applies. I have gained things that I regretted losing; and I know that things will get even better. Whatever reasons you had, it doesn't matter. The important thing is that we are here, and now I come to find out that you are another part of my family. This is absolutely wonderful!"

Dr. P was speechless. Of all the times he had agonized in his sleep, not telling his friend and co-worker of their actual connection, then blaming himself for Evan's death, this confession seemed much too easy. He felt like he was really being let off the hook without having to do any type of suffering or penance – it almost didn't seem fair.

Evan saw the angst on Mark's face. He put down his food, looked the doctor square in the eye, and said these words:

"What has happened before is being undone; we're moving in the same direction now. Let's just enjoy our time here; let's enjoy our families and the shared experience of bringing new life to this corner of our new, mind-altering reality. Every day, it's like saying 'hello' to youth".

"Wow! That was eloquent!" Mark marveled. "I had no idea that backing out of a lie could be so easy. But now that it's done, I won't ever have to worry about it again!"

Evan gave him a re-assuring look. "Walter has already taught me a lot", he said. "What I am figuring out on my own is that lies are eventually erased and vanish away; sickness fades, and despair has no permanent residence – it's *all* good."

"You do realize, of course" Mark reminded him, "that all of this eventually goes away. At some point, we'll stop caring about things and other people and just focus on ourselves – we will start to become a lot more selfish. I still don't understand how that's all a part of becoming perfect!"

The two men looked at each other and paused to find the next set of words to offer each other. They came with some difficulty; part of the magic of their relationship was cemented in the work they did – fellowship was shared, not necessarily spoken. As they prepared to separate once again to work among the furrows of the field, Dr. P's eyes suddenly brightened, and he said:

"Hey, by the way, I'm taking you to a special place for dinner tonight. I already talked to your family and told them I would be stealing you away. They'll be having dinner at my house with the rest of my – er – *our* family, so don't worry about them."

"And is there some special reason that YOU are taking ME out to dinner?" Evan chuckled. He was attempting to make a joke, although he was rather intrigued.

"It's a special gathering; it's where all the doctors go for dinner", Mark countered. "Pretty soon, your whole family will be joining in, and you'll get accustomed to this most wonderful part of our job – the part where we get to say our final goodbyes to the families we helped to reunite."

Evan scratched his head and looked puzzled. "I don't have any idea what you're talking about."

His friend clapped him on the back and started to walk away. Looking back over his shoulder, he yelled back, "You will, Evan … you will."

Addy and Craig made their way the relatively short distance to the Pickford cottage. Although she didn't know exactly what topics of conversation would come up, she was glad the information that both families were actually related had already been unloaded.

Oddly enough, she guessed that Craig had already figured it all out. He was bright way before his years; almost as bright as the evening sun, setting in the east. It was amazing how the next day would promise the permanent erasure of another day of memories – some good, some bad – but it was another day she would gladly give up, because her two men were back with her. For the first time since her arrival in *Backstep*, she was no longer afraid of going to sleep – she truly knew that the nightmares which had awaited her so often would now finally melt away. As her features changed gradually into that of a carefree, happy young woman, she knew that life was good … and getting better.

As for Evan, life was getting much, much better; so quickly, in fact, that it was hard to keep things in perspective. Coming into the Great Hall, Mark made his way through the doorway first, followed by his partner and the other doctors from the East Field. Evan didn't recognize any of the faces of the people around him; on the other hand, all the other doctors were instantly acknowledged and applauded. Feeling a little embarrassed, Evan made his way among the crowd, toward the head table. Mark had explained to him just a little of what he could expect; however, Evan was only an observer on this night. He followed Mark, David and Justin as they waded through a hero's welcome. Jake came in a little later – he was cordial, although he clearly wanted to be somewhere else. They were polar opposites – Jake only had a few more of these dinners to attend; on the other hand, Evan was just becoming accustomed to his new nightly ritual.

Once the doctors had all been seated, there was a loud banging on the front table. One of the elders rose to speak, garnering the attention of everyone with his deep, booming voice.

"Ladies and gentlemen, I bid you all welcome" he started. "This is a very special night. We want to offer our heartfelt 'thank you's to the people who have brought members of our families together. After tonight, none of you will remember the day of your harvest. For all of us, once again, it will be like saying 'hello' to youth …"

A cold chill instantly ran down Mark's spine. These were the very words he had heard Evan say earlier, and he wracked his brain to try and decide whether it was just coincidence or whether perhaps this phrase held some sort of deeper meaning. Shaking it off, he prepared for his speech: as the honored guests, the doctors each addressed the crowd after dinner – they rotated the honor of serving as the keynote address speaker. Tonight, the rotation had made its way around to Mark, and he had a good idea about what he wanted to say.

After a scrumptious meal, Evan was briefly introduced as the newest doctor to arrive at *Backstep*. None of the people recognized him because he was not there when these families experienced their own ordeals – soon, however, things would change for Evan.

David and Justin were the next to speak. The words they offered were kind; neither spoke for very long. Evan noticed that everything sounded so much alike, it was almost as if one had borrowed the speech from the other and simply altered it a little bit. Jake was the next to speak; consequently, it was nearly a fiasco. In much the same way that he was becoming distracted in his work, he was also growing more sarcastic in his tone and mannerisms.

Evan tried to pay attention to what each of the men said, but his own thoughts continued to drift toward Addy – and now, to know that this man, his friend and colleague, was actually a member of his family! He did his best to search the recesses of his brain to see if there were any points of recognition carried over from his previous life … at any time, had he ever suspected that Mark and Addy were brother and sister? How could he have known? … But then, as close as he was to both individuals, how could he NOT have known?

Finally, Mark stood. He glanced at Evan, gave him a wink, then cleared his throat and began addressing the crowd:

"My dear friends, we have all gained something in this past week. Some of us had been tortured with dreams, but all of us were prepared for a new arrival. Well, those arrivals are still in our consciousness, but tomorrow they will be gone. After tonight, we will look into each other's faces and we will smile and greet each other warmly; however, the story will no longer be written. As it should be, our minds are working in reverse, and we do things a little more simply every day. The loved ones you see around you are not growing old, they are growing young. Some are already living fast and running free; for others, time merely waits."

"Personally, I have been given a unique gift. A few days ago, I was joined by a friend, after a long period of separation. This man's name is Evan Alexander (Mark pointed toward Evan). Not only did I need him as a professional colleague, but I also needed him to help correct a few things in my previous life – things that only he could help me with. Now that he is here, things can start to move forward for me."

"Friends, what I would like to say to you is this -- although, like everything else, these words will leave your memory after a brief while: Don't worry about your faults; they will all vanish before you leave this place … your anger will go, your families will cement their bonds, sins will be removed and the things that in a previous life you lamented over never being able to take back, you will be able to. I now raise my class and offer a toast – to my friend, to all my colleagues, to family who couldn't be with me tonight, but most of all – to all of you … Here's To The 'Light of Pureforth'."

"The Light of Pureforth!" The people accepted the toast, drank from their glasses and offered up a very emotional ovation. After he had finished, Mark made his way to the door; the other doctors followed. They made a receiving line, to greet the people as they left. Evan noticed it was almost the exact opposite of when they had arrived. Now, all the families were being saluted by the doctors, for one final time.

Evan stood behind Mark's right shoulder; he was really not a part of the receiving line, although he did smile and wave at many of those who passed by. He was puzzled about this final part of the ritual, but Mark would later go on to explain that this was like their final release into the world – this was akin to the doctor cutting the umbilical cord between a baby and a birthing mother in the old world. After tonight, these people would never have a need for a harvester again … until a new family member came along!

Chapter 13: Hitting His Stride

The two doctors worked side by side, day in and day out. After nearly a week of doing this together, Evan had really begun to hit his stride. Mark marveled at his work and at how effectively he was able to resolve some of the conflicts that came up, periodically. However, as they continued getting younger, their best days of caring for their arrivals were leaving them behind, little by little. They were still very good at what they did, but they seemed to be more easily distracted by trivial things. Jake was becoming more of a hindrance than a help, and almost everyone was happy that he would be leaving soon. He tried really hard, but he seemed clumsy and inept as a doctor. Mark knew that, someday, that would be him.

As they crossed paths in the field, Evan shot a quick glance in Mark's direction and announced: "Well, tonight's the night – I'm bringing the whole family!"

"All except for Craig" Mark reminded him. "We're saving that for tomorrow night."

Evan wondered aloud: "But how will that all work out? I am a doctor, yet tonight I am one of the celebrants because this marks one week since my arrival. Will I be up at the head table still?"

"Enough with the questions already … you'll see. Right now, we have a very important delivery to make. You might recognize her; then again, you might not.

The doctors strode together to the southwest corner of the field. A fairly large group had gathered -- occasionally, when a larger group assembled, the doctors realized that this was a more significant delivery for the people of Backstep, for whatever reason.

As they greeted the extended family, Mark grabbed one of the men by the hand and said, "Your mother meant so much; and now, we'll all have a chance to see and appreciate her work again – she was quite a woman, in the old world."

Evan and Mark worked together for the delivery; fortunately, things in the field had quieted down enough to where they both could help. Evan was glad because it was apparent that this delivery was an important one. He didn't recognize the face of the woman, at first; the creases in the skin seemed full of worry and anguish. He guessed that she was in her forties, which meant she would not ever get to become a teacher. Evan did most of the work covering the woman with the customary purple sheeting, then providing instructions for the rest of the family. Despite Mark's clue, Evan still couldn't quite put the puzzle pieces together.

After a couple of hours, the lady was led off by one of the stewards of the field. As she walked into the distance, Mark came over to where Evan was standing – the two of them looked on as the woman, steadied by a younger lady, eventually vanished from view. Mark decided to test Evan's intuition.

"Did you notice anything familiar about her?" he inquired.

"Oh, is this another one of your little games, pal?" asked Evan.

"No, pal! I am just wondering if you noticed anything about that woman – because she is very important."

"Okay, I give up. I didn't see anything about her that I might recognize."

"Well, you wouldn't" replied Mark. "Some of her facial features changed a lot during her last few weeks. She used to be one of our colleagues."

"You mean that's –"

"Yes; that would be Vivian …"

Evan tried to remember her face. During her last few weeks at the hospital, things had been extremely busy. Despite her cancer, Vivian Workman had bravely tried to continue working her caseload, fighting through the pain and exhaustion, but she believed in her work and she was definitely not a quitter. Sometimes, other doctors would cut corners to try and speed things up, and Vivian never liked that. She spoke harsh words to some of the doctors, on occasion. The last words she had spoken to Evan were harsh, but they were simply in the heat of the moment. In the old world, people often said things that they really didn't mean, but then found themselves in situations where they couldn't take back the hurtful things they said … some would be carried around as dreadful burdens for the rest of their lives.

Suddenly, Evan thought back to the anger and dread he had experienced when he first arrived in Backstep. Much of that anger had subsided, especially since he had been reunited with Addy and Craig. After tonight, the source of that anger would be completely gone – that tortuous nightmare would no longer enter his mind when the nighttime came. He wondered what kind of nightmare Vivian might have had before she arrived. Evan was also a little curious about how different her mannerisms might be, upon her return.

When they had finally finished their work for the day, Mark and Evan cleaned up and changed clothes, then made their way to the Great Hall. Terri and Addy joined them there, along with their families. The only one missing was Craig – he was still a little too weak to make these ventures; however, he was getting stronger every day. Tomorrow he would finally get the chance to join in with them for dinner; then, they would be together, for good.

Evan began to explain to Addy some of the formalities of the dinner, and what their individual roles would be; he had attended five of them now, and he was quickly approaching the time when his memory would only be filled with days of work and nights of celebration. As he barked instructions to Addy in a quite animated fashion, she simply smiled and nodded her head. Terri had already filled her in on all the details, but both women realized that this was the moment for their husbands to shine; so they simply sat back, shared in the joy, and reveled in the fact that they were all united – but this time, not just the two men as professional colleagues, but both families in their entirety – one big, happy, extended family … the way it *should* have been in the old world.

The doctors and their families strolled into the room. David and Justin were first, followed by several other doctors that Evan had met, but only briefly. Mark and Evan were wedged in the middle, followed by a few more doctors. At the very end of the line was Jake.

Immediately, when he entered the Hall, a huge ovation rippled through the crowd. This was his last night with them; he had worked as a doctor for about thirty-three years and tonight, as a twenty-two year old, he and his long-time girlfriend were departing this stage of life. He was concentrating more and more on reading and book learning, and on being in love. Jake seemed to be a very restless soul, but he was very caught-up in the circumstances of his celebrity; and he appeared very proud to share this with Lucille Patterson, who idolized his sweet charm and his dark good looks. The rotation to serve as the keynote speaker had fallen to him, and it was only fitting since tonight would be the very last time he would participate in these proceedings.

The meal was exquisite, as usual. There was idle chitchat among the group of fifteen doctors at the head table – they varied in ages from fifty-one to Jake. Mark and Evan were nestled right in the middle, in terms of age. The realization was there that, with Jake's departure, they would be one doctor short; however, there was an unspoken group acknowledgement that for the past few days they had been working more *around* Jake than with him. Every day, he tried really hard; but lately, he was making many mistakes that an experienced doctor just wouldn't make … mistakes that he never made himself, when he was older.

All else seemed forgotten now; the other doctors were happy for him, now that he was free to leave one stage of his journey toward perfection and begin totally focusing on another. His love for book learning would eventually fade, as would his love for Lucille. But, unlike in the old world, these endings would not be unhappy ones – they would simply melt into other pleasantries and diversions, as he continued to grow younger and more filled with restless energy.

Finally, the time came for the ceremony to begin. Throughout the evening, individuals made their way up to the head table to greet each doctor, re-introducing themselves and offering thanks for the delivery of a precious family treasure. Evan remembered many of the faces and names – it was much easier to do when you only had to go back seven days, and no further.

The crowd turned its attention to Jake as he stood to address them. It had been almost two weeks since he had given his last speech, so he couldn't remember the words he had said before; not that it really mattered, because this was a brand new group of people and it was the only departure speech that many of them would ever hear, much less remember. As he steadied himself and nervously took a sip of water, he gazed toward Lucille, who smiled a very adoring smile.

"My friends" he began, "thank you for this wonderful evening and the chance to once again see all of you together. It is an honor for me to speak to you tonight, because just as this is your chance to pay honor to all of us, to which we are grateful, it is my chance to pay honor to all of my other colleagues, who have shown me so much and to whom I owe a huge debt of gratitude."

He then proceeded to hold a little bit of a "roast", poking fun at various colleagues and sharing a few funny stories of things that had happened over the course of the past week. Jake's talk was lively and entertaining; no one seemed the least bit bored throughout his free-flowing delivery. As he listened, Evan wondered what words he might say the following night, when it was his turn to speak; however, for right now, he (like everyone else) just sat back and let Jake have his final moment in the setting sun of his professional life.

" … and so, I would like to leave you all with this thought – and you can try to hold onto it as much as you like, but it'll be gone in seven days, so don't worry – but here it is:

Being young is a wonderful thing, but it's something that none of us has to worry about. If you lived long enough before, you become younger now … as you become younger, a little bit more of your knowledge goes away, but so do a lot of your cares, worries and anxieties. I can't even begin to tell you what I worried about ten years ago or twenty years ago; all I know is that, right here, right now, I know what's around me and I know what I want. My eventual destiny will be penned in the ink of perfection, but I've got a long way to go before that pen is finally removed from its well. As for now, I relinquish my care to my two dear parents."

With that, he stretched his arms out and a man and woman (perhaps in their late fifties) made their way forward to embrace their son. There were no tears of joy, and there were no regrets. It seemed to be the way, in *Backstep*: in most cases, when there was an emotional moment, it usually swayed more toward the happy than the sad. Sadness, although present in this land, was something that could be dealt with and then released; people here could not carry it around with them for longer than a day. Even the dreams that haunted many of them in the night, as a reminder of the pain and suffering that existed in the old world, would be wiped away by a new day, a warm sunlight and the promise of another step closer toward being perfect.

After the dinner and the speech and several more cordial exchanges, the people began to disperse. The next time they saw each other on the streets, they might recognize names and faces, but the bond that brought them all together on this night would be forever erased from their minds. Even Jake, who might miss being in the field for the first day or two, would soon forget his connection to this place, and concentrate on other things (as he had already started to do).

Just as he was making his way out of the Hall, Evan felt an arm grab him. He stopped and turned to face a man, in his late twenties.

"You may not remember me very well" the man said. "My name is Craig … Craig Whitehouse."

"Oh yes, Craig, I remember you … you happened to be my very first harvest!"

Evan's eyes brightened, because he was just then hit with the realization of the importance of his job.

"Well, there is no need to thank me, Craig. Seeing you reunited with your family is thanks enough."

"Actually, I didn't come to thank you. I wanted to ask for your forgiveness."

"Forgiveness? For what?"

Craig's upper lip stiffened. He wanted to get these words out quickly, and be done with them. He wanted to forget as much as he could, as quickly as he could.

"Very soon", he said, "the harvesting field is going to change. You will notice lots of little boys and girls being pulled up out of the ground. It's going to mean a lot of extra work for you and the other doctors … and it will all be because of me."

"But I don't understand", Evan puzzled.

"All I can tell you is that I did some horrible things in my life", Craig admitted. "Now, I'm in a position to oversee the reversal of all those deeds. You and I will not have this conversation again, and we will both forget its contents. But you will see me near the field when each and every one of these children is extracted. I will not be with the families; I will simply be an onlooker … it is a part of what I have to do in my first few days here."

Evan didn't quite understand, and he tried to brush off this somewhat morbid stranger and move on to more joy and happiness.

"Well, whatever it was – I'm sure it couldn't have been that bad … listen, you just enjoy the evening, get a good night's sleep, and enjoy all the thoughts and possibilities that are part of a bright future!"

Craig wanted to say more, but stopped short. He had said what he needed to; but he hadn't considered whether Evan would accept his words, probe further into their dark meaning, or even how the doctor might react. What he got, in return, was not as much acknowledgement or compassion as he had hoped for. He worried about how Evan (and the other doctors) might behave toward him if they saw him constantly popping up near the edge of the harvesting field.

As they were leaving for their homes, Mark caught up with Evan.

"Who was that strange man who grabbed you, near the door? he asked.

"The man identified himself as Craig … Whitehouse, I believe was his last name. Funny, isn't it? My first harvest happened to be someone with the same first name as my own son!"

"What did he want?"

"Strangely enough, he wanted to apologize to me … for something that hasn't even happened yet."

Mark's eyebrows lowered. "Well, that's rather odd."

"Yeah, I can't really make sense of it either. He did say that he would be making frequent visits to the East Field, however. I don't know why, but I do remember getting a really strange vibe when we delivered him up last week."

"Oh, that's the guy!" Mark suddenly perked up. "I remember now. Yes, that was a bit of a weird delivery. Even though the occasions are usually quite euphoric, I did notice that particular one seemed to be filled with a sense of the macabre. It was really very unnerving."

"Well, whatever the circumstances were that revolve around his entry into this place, things can only get better for him, I suppose", Evan pondered.

"Yes, some things are probably best left alone, for the present".

As the two doctors and their families walked off to their respective homes, Craig Whitehouse quietly watched. He had come as close as he was allowed toward making a confession to one person; and the person that he picked was the very doctor who had delivered him. Now, his life simply had to play itself out, in reverse. The horrible deeds that he hinted at had already been done. Now, he was simply a bystander who could only watch as loved ones were reunited in this new land. He was no longer held responsible; but he continued to feel guilt and remorse. He would see things happen, but only be a part of them indirectly. For now, silent observation was to be his punishment.

Chapter 14: Changes Brewing

With each passing day, the residents of *Backstep* readily accepted their fate – if you could call it that. If fate was something that could be held in your hands one day, and then when you picked it back up the next day it seemed younger, more supple, more vibrant – then that was something these people could adjust to very quickly ... most of them, anyway.

Evan was trying to grapple with a lot of new concepts at once. On the one hand, he enjoyed having his family around him. He had forgotten how much he had missed Addy's companionship – now that he was no longer haunted by those nightmarish images during his sleep, his dreams had transformed into thoughts of Craig running around, cancer-free and quite happy.

Craig – his son! What an amazing young man he was! Though he tried unsuccessfully to remember back, Evan believed that he never really appreciated the unflappable spirit that his boy had shared with the world during his brief stay. Now that they had been reunited, he wanted to make sure that he paid more attention to his son and took more of a solid interest in the things he was involved with. He was very happy that Walter had been able to help secure a "job" for the young man – working over at the hospital, with the kids in the cancer wing. By sharing his sense of humor and bringing smiles to the faces of all the kids (and their families), Evan was convinced that this was just the type of medicine that would result in the cancer being driven from Craig's body even sooner. The fact that it would go away eventually was inevitable; but Craig now had a job to keep spirits high, and to truly help others.

His thoughts then shifted to Mark. Before, he was just a professional partner; now, he had become a member of the family. As much as he tried to rationalize, Evan could feel a certain presence within his mind that Mark could actually read his thoughts; sometimes, he believed he could read what was going through Mark's brain, as well. Could it be possible that two men, not related, could have developed some type of extra-sensory perception that linked their two brains together? In this new land, lots of things were possible that could have never worked in the old world. As Evan continued to ponder this matter, he considered the new "senses" he had developed as a harvesting doctor. Where had these unique gifts come from? Was there something special he would eventually have to do in return for this wonderful new power that he now possessed?

Family matters, however, were not the only changes brewing within. Evan was encountering lots of new people. As their first point of contact with the new world, he was making an indelible mark on them. Some seemed to recognize him; others acknowledged his importance in society; still others displayed anger, an emotion he understood because remnants of his initial rage still lived within him, if nothing more than to constantly remind him of how dark things can be for some people at certain points in their lives. Several times he had asked Walter about this – the older man simply said that there are "some things that we can't fully understand, but we just have to accept".

Each new workday promised a fresh set of souls, and laid the foundation for more stories that the teachers would unveil to their students, in due time. Evan's thoughts traced themselves back to Vivian, who would eventually be making her first working visit to the East Field.

"What was the cruel thing that she said to me?" Evan tried to piece it together, and he wondered when Vivian might return. When she did, he wondered how he might behave toward her. He certainly had more of an appreciation for people with cancer – Craig had already taught him much about that in the short time that had passed since the two of them had arrived here.

As soon as the name Craig entered his mind, memories resurfaced from the night before – and the strange man who had grabbed his arm at the Great Hall. He knew that the first name was Craig, but trying to remember him by this name caused a great deal of confusion. There could only be one Craig in his life, so this man would have to be known by another name.

"Let's see, his last name was … Whitehouse! Therefore, from now on, I will simply refer to him as 'Whitehouse'".

It seemed like a very easy resolution, and Evan felt better now, knowing that whenever he thought of the stranger with the dark secret that he wouldn't have to mix it with feelings of his own son. How weird that one name could cause so much joy and yet so much pain at the same time! He was better off, he thought, keeping these two people (and their corresponding images) as far apart as he could.

When he arrived at the East Field, Mark was already there – he seemed to invariably run a little early, whereas Evan had a tendency to run behind schedule, a little.

"There you are!" Mark cried out. "I didn't think, at first, that you would be coming in today."

Evan tried to think of something quick to say in return. Actually, he was feeling a little embarrassed for running late, especially since they would be one doctor short that day.

"I just thought I would make you panic a little bit, because Jake is no longer around!"

"What are you talking about? He was never here, even when he *was* here!"

It was a sharp thing to say, but both men laughed. They had been stepping over and around Jake for the past few days, and they were relieved that they wouldn't have to go through that today. Even though Jake had moved on, Evan and Mark did not envy him – they couldn't think of anything else they would rather be doing than harvesting souls during the day, then celebrating with friends and family at night.

"I can't wait to get started" Mark gushed. "For some reason, I was just really anxious to get to work today."

"I'm a little excited too" admitted Evan. "Part of my excitement, however, deals with later on … I'll finally get a chance to introduce Craig to other members of the community."

"Don't be so sure that other people don't already know Craig … and quite well, I might add!"

It was true. In the brief time that he had been making visits to Childrens' Hospital, the boy had already made a name for himself. Kids were calling for him in their sleep, and his infectious humor had already become the stuff of legend. Because he was so busy with his own work, Evan could not witness it firsthand; but every night, Addy would regale him with stories of how Craig had led a parade through the halls of the intensive care unit, or how he was able to engage some of the kids in jumping contests on the tops of their beds, or create some spur-of-the-moment game, such as "Pin The

Tail On The Adult". Mere thoughts of these things made Evan chuckle; he then realized that as famous as he himself might be to the members of this society, his son just might outshine them all.

Midway through the morning, Addy and Craig stopped by the field. Seeing them, Evan quickly completed another delivery and made his way over.

"What are you two up to?" he chided, playfully.

"Craig decided to take a little break, so we're going over to Sophia's hill. I hear she is a wonderful storyteller and Craig and I could use a little entertainment right now."

"What, you mean the youngster is not enough entertainment by himself?"

"Oh, you know what I mean, silly! Everyone needs a break every now and then. Besides, don't you want him all rested and refreshed for the big night tonight?"

"I was only kidding" Evan replied. "You two go ahead and Mark and I will catch up with you later ... you know, your brother is a pretty neat guy; I'm very glad that we are all part of the same family!"

A tear welled up in the corner of Addy's eye. "Oh, I'm so happy", she responded. She wanted to say more, but stopped short. One secret had been revealed, and that was enough for now ... so far, so good. But the thing that remained for her to tell her partner would prove to be much more difficult. It was the one thing that continued to haunt her in her dreams. Now that Evan and Craig had come back, and Mark had been brought into the family fold, the burdens seemed to be lifting. But how could she share the one thing that only three other people in her life knew about?

As they walked away, Mark's eyes strayed toward the west end of the field. A stranger was standing there, alone. Looking closer, Mark recognized the face.

"Hey, isn't that the guy who grabbed you by the arm last night?"

Evan looked over. Indeed it was ... it was – Whitehouse! But what was he doing here? He had just been harvested a few days earlier. Was he already back to claim another family member? Could this have something to do with the eerie revelation he made the night before?

The man motioned for Evan. Hesitant at first, Evan pointed at himself, as if there was a possibility that the man had been trying to gain someone else's attention instead. The man confirmed his wants with a slow nod of the head, and Evan cautiously made his way over to where the man stood.

"Are you here to claim someone?" Evan asked nervously, although he seemed to know that this was not the reason for the man's visit.

"Not exactly. Listen closely – you must do exactly as I say. Before you begin your next delivery, go get the older doctor (he gestured with his head over to where Justin was standing). This will be unlike any delivery you have made so far, and it could get messy. The older doctor will know what to do; he will help you."

Craig looked straight into Evan's eyes, as he continued: "I will be standing here watching, but you must do nothing to draw any attention to me, whatsoever. I can't tell you anything more; you simply have to trust me – I have no reason to lie to you."

Evan felt a cold chill run down his spine. He believed every word that the man told him, and as he made his way over to the northeast corner, where a large crowd was starting to gather, he felt a sense of both dread and terror. He motioned for Justin to assist him. As soon as Justin saw the crowd and detected the apprehension in Evan's eyes, he called for someone to finish up the job he was in the middle of, and rushed over to help his colleague.

Before they arrived at the ever-growing throng, Justin suddenly stopped and stared at Evan, who was carrying one purple cloak.

"Don't make a big scene, but grab another one, too" he said. "… and have someone bring lots of towels."

Evan did all that was asked of him and then joined Justin at the bustling corner of the field. There was so much anticipation that the doctors felt their adrenaline pumping more than they had ever felt before. Evan stepped forward and asked the question:

"Are you the parents?"

The young couple stepped forward. Evan guessed that they were in their thirties, although their worn features betrayed their ages. Dark, puffy circles encased their red eyes – it was obvious that there had been a great deal of crying and restless nights previous to this event.

"Yes, we are ready." They gripped each others' hands tightly, and turned away from where Justin was kneeling. Evan calmly gave them the instructions, and the man and woman closed their eyes and began to hum. He asked some of the others who had assembled to close ranks around them, forming a little huddle, and encouraged them to hum along.

Once they had started their song, Evan dropped to one knee and noticed that Justin was tending to not one head, but two – one was pushing out of the ground a little faster than the other.

"Whatever you do, just make sure they don't turn around!" Justin whispered between tightly clenched teeth. "This could get really ugly, really quickly!"

As Evan bounced back and forth between the older doctor and the nearly delirious couple, Justin worked feverishly to fish out the two bodies – the first was the little girl, perhaps only eight years old. After she was cleaned and neatly wrapped, safe and secure in the purple cloak, Justin completed the delivery of the younger brother, who may have been only five or six. There was a great deal of blood present, more than Evan had ever seen; but Justin was able to handle everything masterfully. Although he was sweating profusely, he finished up in a very casual manner, and motioned for Evan to turn the family around and give them instructions – to take their children home.

Immediately, Jane Latrelle collapsed to the ground between the two children, face down on the ground, with her left arm spread across one child and her right spread across the other. Her uncontrolled sobs washed over the ground beneath her face, and her partner Rowan clutched her tightly as she continued to heave and grasp at her two lost treasures. After what seemed like an eternity, Jane looked up and kept gasping the same words, over and over: "Thank you … thank you … thank you …"

She stroked the hair of her children and bathed their faces with her tears and kisses. Although they weren't yet conscious, they both seemed to be resting very peacefully – far removed from whatever forces had brought them to this place.

Quite a few of the people had dispersed, now that the show was over. The mother and father remained. Evan made several attempts to get them to return home, but Jane was adamant about staying. He understood that, under certain circumstances, rules could be bent a little bit …

and this woman did not look like she was going to be easily separated from her children. Evan looked toward the woman's partner and said:

"Stay as long as you need to. I need to go and make more deliveries, but Catherine is right here (he motioned toward the young intern). If you need anything, just ask … as soon as we can release the children into your care, we will."

"Thank you, doctor" the grateful father managed to blurt out. "We'll be going soon, but Jane just needs a little more time."

"I understand", Evan said. With those words, he placed a hand on Rowan's shoulder, offered a pat, then walked away. Greatly relieved, he walked toward the center of the field, where Mark caught up with him.

"Wow, I've never seen one of those before – a double delivery! No wonder the crowd was so big."

He didn't ask any more questions about the procedure, which kind of puzzled Evan, who thought this was one great story that should become an instant classic, that people would talk about for a long, long time … and yet, Mark was hardly paying it any attention.

"Hey, by the way, what did that Whitehouse fellow want?"

Evan's attention suddenly shot back to the strange visitor. He desperately looked around, but he was nowhere to be found.

"How did he know?" Evan loudly questioned.

"How did who know what?" Dr. P asked.

"Oh, never mind. I'm just becoming more and more curious about that Whitehouse fellow. He said something to me before the delivery that was a little puzzling, and I'm just trying to make sense of it all."

"Well, you better not try too hard … I don't think your next customer will expect anything less than your complete and undivided attention!" Mark motioned toward the opposite end of the field where an elderly woman was waiting, very impatiently. With her hands on her hips, tapping her left foot to the ground, she fixed her stare on Evan as he made his way over to where she stood.

"It sure took you long enough" she stormed. "Well, now that you're here, let's get on with this mess!"

Evan gave the instructions to Maylene Souther, who then turned around. She seemed very bothered by every little detail of this episode in her life, almost as if it was an absolute waste of her time. It was very odd to the doctor about how callous and unfeeling this woman appeared to be.

The delivery did not take long. She took one look at the old man lying on the ground, and she said "Yep, that's him alright; that's Bud … I suppose you'll just send him home when you're done with him."

… and with that, she walked off. Evan was absolutely stunned. He watched the woman walk away, without the least bit of an emotional response, then cast another glance over at the Latrelles, who were still caught up in the euphoria of being reunited with their children.

He thought about how Addy reacted when he had first arrived, and about his family's response to their little boy when he made his initial appearance in the field.

"How strange and how different we all are" he marveled to himself. "I guess perfection is a lot further away for some of us than it is for others." With those words, Evan washed his hands and headed for his next task.

Chapter 15: Missing Persons

The dinner was a nice change of pace for Evan, on what had otherwise been a very hectic and confusing day. Terri and the children joined Addy and Craig, and all the doctors and their families strode into the Great Hall. Craig was instantly captivated by the large number of people, the flickering lights of the candles, and all the food that was laid out before them. As he looked on, he began to feel so full that he believed he could not eat one single bite ... that's when he knew it was going to be a very good meal indeed.

Evan settled in next to Addy at the table; Craig nestled in next to her on the other side. The evening's conversation was light. Addy playfully admonished Craig, as he and Alex unveiled their little mischievous antics. As was customary, various individuals made their way up to the table to thank the doctors for their work. He had seen it a few times already, but Evan was still amazed about the constant genuflections by the people toward the doctors.

"After all" he thought, "...we are only performing a service, like everyone else does ... and yet, the people revere us as if what we are doing is the most important thing in the world."

Whether he was thinking those thoughts aloud or not, he wasn't sure; but suddenly, to his left, Mark leaned in and whispered in his ear:

"To them, right now, what we have done is not just the most important thing in the world ... it is, in fact, their *whole* world!"

"Can you really read my thoughts, or am I just thinking out loud?"

"Perhaps a little of both" Mark responded. "It doesn't matter though; we can just make that our little secret."

Evan thought for a moment. "So you know what went on with me out there in the field today … with those two children?"

"I know *what* happened; I just don't know *why*. When I talked to Justin, he told me that he had handled several deliveries like that before, but not very often. He also told me that you did very well, and that you were a 'natural' to start handling the really complicated ones that we get from time to time."

"But how did *he* know?"

"How did *who* know?"

Evan stiffened. "You know … the guy … Whitehouse. He was there today. He called me over, gave me some instructions, watched for a few minutes and then he was gone. There is something very strange about him; but I still can't quite put my finger on it.

"Well, don't worry about it" Mark reassured him. "The important thing is that those children are back with their families, and order has been restored once again."

With those words, Mark began eating, and he urged his working companion to do the same. Evan fell into his meal, and soon his mind diverted to his speech. He knew what he wanted to say; he just hoped all the words would come out the way he intended them to. It was a very special night for him. His whole family was back together; and now, he was going to have his first real opportunity to publicly thank all his loved ones. As the moment lingered, Evan saw one of the elders approach the center of the head table, and begin with the more formal part of the program.

"It is my pleasure to introduce to you one of our fine doctors" he said. "Although he has been with us only a short time, to many of you in this room he has already been here an eternity. Ladies and gentlemen, I present Doctor Evan Alexander!"

Greeted by loud applause and cheers, Evan rose to deliver his speech to the audience. The name suddenly struck him full – he didn't remember ever having been addressed as 'Doctor Evan Alexander' before. The name sounded rich and powerful; and yet, at this moment, he felt very small and humble. He shook off the cobwebs that shrouded his brain, and began to speak.

"Dear friends, and honored guests", he began. "Tonight is both an ending and a beginning. For the past week, many of you have contemplated what you would think, say or feel here in this room. I suppose I can understand that, because recently I celebrated the one week marking of my own arrival. One thing I have discovered, however, is that the bond of family is stronger than perhaps any other force that we know of. It is stronger than sickness … it is stronger than weakness … it is stronger than sadness."

As he spoke, Evan's words became more forceful and confident. Words streamed from his lips, as he succumbed to their power. He spoke of his love for his partner, he told the crowd all he could remember about cancer and how his own son was a shining example of the amazing possibilities of life. Then, he did something very unexpected: he introduced Craig to the audience.

When Craig stood up, the ovation that ensued was thunderous. Many people already knew about Craig, from his recent work at the hospital. Others simply saw him as a young man in the process of conquering a disease that, previously, had bested him. Craig didn't know whether his dad had wanted him to say anything, although he was never shy. Given the chance, he would have happily stolen the spotlight away, no matter who it was intended for at the time. Now, however, he merely waved to the crowd, sat back down, and relinquished the focus of attention back to his father.

Evan shifted his gaze to a fairly large group of people settled toward the back of the room. Several nuns, wearing bright blue habits, were seated at the table with six people, most of them older. It appeared that none of these people had family members with them – they had formed their own family.

"Some of us in the room may feel like we are missing … we feel like missing persons. Perhaps no direct family members have claimed us yet, or even if they have, we may not feel like we have really become a part of that family. But just remember that, here – in the land of *Backstep* – we are all connected in some way … we are all family, to some degree. None of us has to ever worry about making it to the end on our own. Pleasant dreams…"

When he sat back down, the crowd was momentarily stunned. The power of his final words had virtually taken away their collective breaths. However, when the first applause broke out, it was greeted with great fervor. Very soon, the entire Hall had erupted in a standing ovation, the likes of which had not been seen for quite some time. People from the crowd began streaming over to the table where the nuns and their dinner guests were seated, and there was much hugging and shaking of hands … as well as a few tears.

Addy reached over and grabbed Evan by the arm. She fought back her own tears as she said, "That's about the most beautiful thing I've ever heard. I guess we're all a little lost sometimes; we just don't want to admit it."

Evan then felt a punch to his left shoulder. "Hey, what are you trying to do – start a riot!?" Mark broke out into a huge smile and then patted his friend on the shoulder. His tone then changed and became much more cordial and subdued. "Very nicely done" he said. " … But then, I knew you would do well."

Mark and Terri walked ahead of them, as Addy and Evan strode arm-in-arm down the path, back toward their home. A little further ahead, Alex and Craig continued to play their little games. The evening was warm and pleasant, and the moonlight shone brightly all around.

"Do you ever feel like a missing person?" Addy asked.

Evan stopped and looked directly into her eyes. "Well, I did feel lost when I first got here, I can tell you that" he responded. "But, very quickly, I found my way and I stepped into a role and a purpose. Part of the reason I was able to make such a smooth transition was because of the help of my family. I really meant what I said – I believe the bonds of family are stronger than any other force."

"Do you really believe that?" she asked.

"Well, why wouldn't I?"

"I don't know, sometimes I think there is always *something* missing … something we can never really get back … something that prevents us from being totally complete."

Evan tried to consider the alternatives. "I'm sure that some people feel that way, but I am absolutely sure that the feeling goes away, over time."

"But are you really sure that's how it works?"

"I'm not really sure how anything works", Evan said, "but it all seems to. Every day, I seem to feel better, and we're all getting younger. Craig has gotten better over the course of a week, and I can't even remember that old nasty dream I used to have. No, I would honestly have to say: Every day I become less and less of a missing person."

Clutching his arm a little more tightly now, Addy just nodded her head and tried to shake off the lost and lonely feeling she still had. She began to wonder to herself: "Why do I feel this way? I have gotten everything back that I had ever asked for -- that I had ever wanted … and now that I have it all, I still don't feel right." She was working hard to convince herself that her life was now on steady ground, but she knew what was still hanging out there -- something she couldn't fully come to grips with … that she couldn't reveal – not just yet.

Terri and Mark knew her secret, but they had sworn they would never say anything to anyone. Sometimes, the two women would take long walks and watch the children play.

Addy tried hard every day to keep tabs on one young lady, in particular. She was about twenty years old and her name was Diana. Diana had lived a long life. She had long, raven hair and delicate, fair skin. Her manner was playful, and she always seemed cheerful and kind. The young woman had a fantastic set of parents, who loved her dearly – their whole family seemed to be perfect in every way. For the most part, it was indeed perfect.

Addy remembered herself at about the same age, in the old world. Vaguely, she remembered a terrible mistake she made, which rendered her a beautiful little daughter. She had tried her best to raise the child on her own, but with no father it was extremely difficult. Before the little girl had reached her second year, she made the decision to put the child up for adoption. Feeling a low sense of self-worth, she wanted her child to be able to experience the warmth and love of a stable family. The child was so precious that many families wanted her. When the Greshams came along, Addy knew deep down in her heart that it was the perfect family.

For many years, Addy kept tracking and following Diana. Her parents had told her she was adopted, but Diana was never curious about the forces of biology that brought her into the world.

All that she knew or cared about were the members of her family who were around her each and every day – the ones who cared about her – the ones who *wanted* her. As time went on, Addy met a man and fell in love. He was a good-looking young doctor, smart and funny, and he held all the promise of a good life. The two eventually married, and they had a son. For years, they had lived the life she had always dreamed of; it was filled with laughter and good times.

When he was about nine years old (in his previous life), Craig was diagnosed with cancer. At first, they thought that perhaps they had caught it soon enough and that the boy would be able to fight it off and survive. Twice, the cancer had gone into remission, but the third time it came back, it came on with a vengeance. The cancer tortured and ravaged his body, and there was nothing the doctors could do. Addy's only recollections of this occurred in her nightly dreams, which were now changing altogether. She was glad that these visions were fading into oblivion.

Evan and Addy had watched their son wither away. Evan started drinking and his career started to unravel. The night Craig died, Evan jumped on his motorcycle and took off into the night rain. Within two days, Addy had to bury both a son and a husband.

After that tragic period, she had a few relationships; but she never married again, and never had any more children. Besides her parents and remaining blood relatives, the only other person she had was Diana – but Diana would never actually meet her true mother until the day Addy died … just to say 'thank you'. Addy felt as if she had lived the majority of her life as a wanderer - a 'missing person'. She often wondered how many others out there felt the same way she did, and truly hoped that a life beyond the realm of pain and sadness awaited them on the other side – in a place called *Backstep*.

When they went to bed that evening, Evan had a difficult time going to sleep; so many images were crowding his head. He had finally gotten the opportunity to have his whole family together in the Hall – something they would enjoy for quite some time to come. Craig was getting better all the time. Addy had seemed quite moody that day, flashing in and out, between euphoria and melancholy. The sight of all the missing people being gathered in and embraced by the community truly touched his soul.

However, the one thing that he simply could not get out of his mind was the man who had cast a pall of dread over him: Whitehouse. Evan didn't think that there was anything evil that existed in this land, but for some reason he sensed a dark force of some kind within this man. The name Craig popped into his mind, and he quickly shook it free. There was no way he wanted the name Craig associated with this strange visitor to the East Field. He simply hoped that he wouldn't see this man again, although he had been assured that he would – and he wasn't looking forward to it, one bit.

Addy rolled toward Evan, and propped up on one elbow. "Are you having trouble sleeping?" she asked. "Maybe I could mix up some of that special tea for you – that may help."

"No, I'm fine" Evan said, as he put his arm around her. "I just … sometimes, I just … wonder."

"What do you wonder?"

"I wonder why we're here. It seems that if we've already lived one life, there's no real need to live the same life in reverse. What does it accomplish?"

Addy thought for a moment. "I think it gives us an opportunity to make up for lost time with our loved ones. Like you said in your speech – here, it's all about family. In the old world, I think it was mostly about the 'I'. How much can *I* do? How much can *I* accomplish? How much money can *I* make?"

Considering what she had just said, Evan looked deep in her eyes. "Do you ever remember what *you* were really about?"

"Yes and no", she cautiously answered. "There were times in my life when I was very much in control, and other times when I was reeling out of control. As long as you and Craig were around, I couldn't have been happier."

"Even when he was sick?"

"Especially when he was sick, believe it or not."

"Oh, I believe you", said the doctor. He continued on:

"You know, when the words came out of my mouth about the 'missing persons', something struck a chord deep within me. I don't know what happened, but I just started to feel like something was missing in my life. Walter tells me that we all lose a little bit of our memory every day, and I guess that's what keeps us from going crazy. Perhaps that's the one thing that helps us to really appreciate all the things we have before us."

"Did something happen to you today that brought about this change?"

Evan then proceeded to tell her about Whitehouse and the throngs of people that had gathered at the Field. He told her about the intense feeling of dread that he had, and how confused it made him that this man had the same first name as their own son.

"It's like he has some kind of message to deliver to me, but for some reason we're not connecting. To me, he seems really lost, and it is making *me* feel really lost."

"Maybe you should talk to him about it sometime" Addy concluded.

"Something deep inside tells me I shouldn't" Evan shot back. "Perhaps there are some things we shouldn't try and delve into ... some things that we should just leave alone and let them play out, without any extra help or intervention."

"Well, you just get a good night's sleep and don't worry about those things anymore", Addy said, as she leaned over and kissed him on the cheek.

"Actually, I feel a little better already. Good night, Addy. I love you."

"I love you too, Evan". With that, the two people rolled away from each other – one to dream about his son and the miracle of life revisited; the other to ponder how much longer she could keep her one big secret from her one and only true love.

Chapter 16: Feeling Stronger Every Day

When you are moving in reverse, things seem to move much faster – the sunrises almost seem frenetic, as if to serve as a reminder that time spent is ever-fleeting and that, soon, all memory of the day will be gone. In contrast, Craig lived his life in a much different mindset.

He greeted each new day in the same manner – he saluted the sky, gave a shrill whistle, stretched his arms and then let out an exhilarated exhale ... it was his way of saying:

"I'm not going to let anything slip past me today ... pain or no pain."

So many people in *Backstep* envied the young man for his unsinkable attitude; yes, there may have been others who suffered from cancer along with him, but Craig seemed to take on a sense of personal responsibility to make others forget about their own pain by following his example. He knew that this was not a disease, but merely a condition; in this land, there was a cure for ALL people ... and that cure was simply getting younger. Although he had his good days and his better days (he refused to have bad ones), Craig knew deep down in his heart that he was moving toward perfection and that he would get there soon enough.

He and Addy went to the hospital together. After the first couple of weeks, Addy stopped staying with her son – she would simply drop him off early and meet up with him later in the day ... sometimes back at the hut, other times at whatever mutual meeting point they chose. Addy enjoyed the fact that Craig was becoming more independent and able to make complicated decisions with relative ease; in many ways, he reminded her a lot of Evan, although Evan spent so much time at work that she hardly got a chance to actually see him and spend time with him, except late at night.

More and more, she felt herself sinking into a kind of empty, solitary life, much like the one she left behind, so many years before.

As soon as he would hit the door, the whole atmosphere at the hospital seemed to transform; often, amazingly, bright sunlight would correspond with his entrance through the main door – it was as if he was literally bringing the sun into the building with him.

Craig would make his rounds, greet each and every child in the ward individually, introduce himself to the new patients, and then he would begin organizing the games. He took it upon himself to get everyone worked up and active so that they would be ready for "story time". Many children were exhausted; for some, it was an extreme effort. Craig, however, had his daily agenda and he was a formidable opponent to the forces of gloom and lethargy.

The first part of the day always seemed to fly by and children often forgot about their individual maladies. As they settled into their routine, they simply followed Craig's instructions and they were led anywhere that his will guided them. At the hospital, children all ate small meals, every three hours – just enough to give them energy for their next activity. The meal was usually preceded by a quick nap of about twenty minutes. For some reason, the nap always brought on the full feeling in the stomach, which is how they knew when to eat something.

After the midday meal, Craig would pair up older, stronger children with smaller and/or weaker ones in wheelchairs. They would then proceed to a hillside, where they would do their 'learning' for the day. It was totally at Craig's discretion as to which teachers he would take them to listen to. Although he had his own personal favorites, he did his best to make sure that the children got to hear many different teachers. At the same time, it was extremely important to Craig that the whole group stay together, as much as possible. He wanted to be able to keep an eye on them, and to make sure that everyone understood the meaning or received the full impact of each and every story.

Craig particularly loved taking the others to see and hear Walter. He had developed a very close personal bond with his paternal grandfather and it occurred to him that they shared many of the same ideals and values, which was extremely rare, given the age difference between the two. Whenever Walter would begin to share a story, a portal would open in Craig's mind – he often thought that Walter's thoughts were channeling special messages to him, that only his mind could unlock. It was confusing, invigorating … mesmerizing.

"Today, boys and girls, I am going to tell you a story about a lady named Alice.

Alice was a delightful woman who always liked to go around picking purple flowers. She was friendly to everyone and she had many children and grandchildren. Whatever age she was, she always seemed to enjoy it very much. One thing she always said was, "You can never be too old."

A little girl, wearing a white dress with purple flowers, looked up into the face of the older boy who was pushing her wheelchair.

"You know, I feel the same way that old woman does" she said, with a gleam in her eye.

The young girl's name was Alice.

After dropping Craig off, Addy made her way to the park near the center of the town. It was a place where she spent much of her time, and every day she went for the same reason – to see HER. When she arrived at her destination, Addy would always catch up with her other friends – those about her own age – and they would sit and talk about things … primarily, any trivial matter that they could think of that had occurred over the past seven days – because that represented their whole world.

During the conversations, Addy would always keep a sharp eye out for the slender young woman with the long, dark hair and the ever-happy demeanor. She was always watching out for Diana. As many times as she wanted to go up to her and say a few words, something inside Addy always prevented her from doing it. But knowing that Diana was happy was enough of a consolation for her, right now. She watched as Diana flirted with a young man, perhaps a couple of years older than herself. Diana blushed; Addy wondered if she might ever behave the same way around a young man, as she became younger herself.

One of her friends noticed the blank, distant stare on Addy's face. Linda Bertolli noticed that Addy's attention had been drawn by the young lady with the dark hair and pale skin.

"So that's what young love looks like!" Linda remarked. "I've often been told that when you become young and you fall in love with someone that you start to blush a lot and act really dizzy. I've seen it happen sometimes, and I often wonder if that will ever happen to me."

"Oh, I suppose it will happen to all of us, sooner or later" replied Monica Solomon, another of the friends.

"I wonder if I will fall in love with someone old and fat, and then watch him change before my very eyes" chuckled the plump woman seated next to her. Naomi Perez was a real character and had a sense of humor that people didn't often understand – the way she spoke, however, enabled her to endear herself to most everyone she met. People always felt comfortable around Naomi – despite the disfiguring scar that raked across the right side of her face.

"I think her name is Diana" Monica blurted out. "She comes from that really well-off family that lives on the other side of the hill over there" (she pointed toward a bluish hill, in the distance to their left). "She has a younger sister too, who is about eight now. The little girl's name escapes me, though."

As the women continued their talk, Addy was relieved. With all of them focusing on the young woman simultaneously, Addy's spying wouldn't be so obvious and her intentions would be lost amidst the cackling of hens. Addy enjoyed their company, but so often she wished she could just share time with the one person in her life who she had been separated from … someone who may have seen her around from time to time, but never knew the connection; never knew the secret.

Addy thought to herself "What would happen if I *did* say something to her? Would she believe me?" Then, she thought again: "With the separation, she would lose all knowledge of me again after seven days … so I would have to keep re-introducing myself. That just seems like much too painful of an option. Besides that, I don't know how her parents would react."

She thought long and hard about the consequences that would come along with whatever actions she took. For Addy, it seemed like there was only one prudent course of action: she would simply watch the girl from a distance and wait until the day when the two of them would be reunited. Her nightly dreams reminded her that she was getting closer, yet she was still so very far away. Diana would never, ever really get to know her mother, which was sad. But for Addy – right here, right now – seeing the young lady, happy, carefree and beautiful, was quite enough. She would look forward to another day.

Back in the East Field, Evan was feeling stronger every day. His herculean efforts were marveled by many; no one had ever seen a doctor able to adeptly handle so many cases with such care and speed. He had totally thrown his mind into his work in order to avoid thinking about Craig's cancer – he would be reminded again of the pain, soon enough – around dinner time.

As he worked, he checked-in, periodically, on the new associate who had come to help them. Vivian, his new colleague, had arrived on the scene with cancer, and did her best to work while she raged her own personal war with pain and physical limitations. She worked seemingly beyond her own deficiencies, and became frustrated whenever she had to ask for help or when things didn't turn out the way she expected. Still, Evan felt a very soft spot in his heart for her. He felt shamed around her, for some reason; yet, he didn't know why.

After work, he asked Mark: "Why do you think I always feel guilty around Vivian – like I've done something wrong?"

"Probably because, at some point, you will!" his friend responded.

"What do you mean?"

"Look, you know how this whole thing works. If you're feeling really bad about something, there is always a reason … the closer you get to the resolution, the more intense the feelings are. Then, poof! it all goes away."

"I am just wondering what it is that I am going to say or do that's causing me to feel this way now", Evan fretted.

"Well, there's no need to worry about it … because, whatever it is … it is GOING to happen!"

"I suppose you're right." Evan resigned himself to the fact that he was going to do something that would change the course of his relationship with Vivian – for the better. He just wasn't sure how long he had to wait. As he was finishing up another delivery and cleaning his hands, Mark pointed over his shoulder toward the far edge of the field.

"Someone is trying to get your attention" Mark motioned to his colleague. Evan looked across and saw a man, standing all by himself. As he made his way over, Evan felt like he knew who this person was, although he couldn't recall ever seeing or meeting him before.

The man knew Evan well; knew everything about him. He had studied Evan's mannerisms, and had watched every day from a distance as Evan did his job. Evan never paid attention to him, never knew he was there; but the man known as Whitehouse paid daily visits to the Field; it was just something he was compelled to do. He had to remember Evan's face, and all the good things that he did. He had even heard that Evan had a son named Craig. It made him feel a little better, knowing that there was at least some small thread that connected him with the doctor – the one man who could help relieve him of some of the horrific fragments of his own existence.

As soon as Evan arrived to where Whitehouse stood, he asked the familiar question, which the mysterious stranger answered in the same fashion as he had the last time, over a week before. A sense of worry suddenly washed over Evan as he turned to see another large crowd gathering on the opposite side of the field.

"What is happening?" he thought.

The man gave Evan very simple instructions and directed the doctor over to where the family members stood. A small group of four people, two adults and two children, huddled closely together, with hands tightly clasped and apprehension written all over their faces, as they stood in front of the masses that were assembling. Clutching her two children to her tightly, the woman said:

"We are here for my daughter ... we have come to claim Janie."

"Wait a minute!" Evan recognized this name and then he recognized the family. They were neighbors of his and he recollected the name of the young girl who would be coming to join them on that day. For such a joyous occasion, Evan saw dreadful looks in all their faces and he didn't understand why, at first.

He gave all the proper instructions and made the delivery. As soon as the little girl was covered, the mother pushed past him and threw herself on top of her daughter, smothering her with kisses and bathing her with tears. Over and over, she kept repeating the same words, as she stroked the hair of the eight-year old girl:

"You will never be separated from us again, until things are finally perfect ... I love you so much, little Janie!"

Evan paused for a moment. What connection did that strange man have with this one occurrence? As he desperately sought his memory banks, he found nothing – only a strange feeling that something similar to this had happened before. He wondered if this messenger carried some deep, dark secret with him. Toward the end of the day, Evan asked around, to see if anyone knew who this man was. Several of the doctors and orderlies had recognized him; they had seen him come to the field every day, as a matter of fact. Some even thought he actually worked there, because they saw him so much. One of the younger attendants said that, when asked his name, the man responded by saying, "My name isn't important ... yet."

"What an odd thing to say" Evan thought. Even so, the overwhelming sense of joy that the doctor felt whenever he reunited families overrode any sense of personal doubt he might have about these surroundings or its inhabitants. Shortly after the delivery, the crowd dissipated, and the young father took his other two children away from the scene, leaving the mother alone with her daughter. As Evan looked on, there was something that seemed more and more familiar about the way the mother was caring for the young girl: the way she cried, held her child, stroked her hair -- the way she would simply not leave her side. All these behaviors were eerily reminiscent of another time, but Evan could not recall it exactly.

He had performed numerous deliveries of children over the course of his short-lived career, but this one seemed unique. Children always brought a large crowd to the field, but never before had he ever remembered receiving instructions from a man on one side of the field before going to attend to a group standing at the opposite end of the field. They were so far away from each other, yet connected ... by something.

When the young child was ready for her departure, her mother still would not leave her side; she insisted on traveling with her the whole way, and there was no denying her this right. Evan was glad that the young girl had the companionship of her mother, but instantly worried that perhaps the mother was a little too clingy, too controlling.

"I'm glad things are not like that in my household" he thought. "Everyone kind of comes and goes as he or she pleases, which is the way I think it should be." He wondered what kind of place *Backstep* would be if everyone behaved the same way all the time – if people were all so predictable that there was never any guesswork at all to this thing called life. He chuckled to himself.

"Hey, what are you laughing at?" called out Dr. P.

"Oh nothing ...nothing. I suppose what we have here is a doctor trying to cure things that don't have a cure, and trying to fix things that don't really need fixing."

"That's what life is all about!" Mark agreed. "I often wonder what I would be doing if I wasn't a doctor.

"Me too" echoed Evan. "I think I would probably be a professional athlete" he added. "But you know I could never do that – and it's all because of my stupid left knee!"

"Well, you move around pretty well, for an *old* man", Mark quipped. "Even so, I *still* don't know what it is that I would really want to do, if I weren't doing this."

"You mean, you don't really enjoy doing this!?"

Mark looked him dead in the eye. "It's not that I don't enjoy it ... it's just that ... well, it's hard to explain. I guess I should just do my job, keep my mouth shut, and enjoy my life!

Later that night, as he was lying in bed, awaiting for sleep to take over,

Evan thought about Mark's curious words. He also knew what he simply must do the next day: he needed to pay closer attention and watch for the stranger who made his daily visits to the field. Evan was going to make it a point to find out more about him, and about why he came there every day. He didn't know what that might accomplish, but he felt that if he didn't do this, several critical questions would remain unanswered. Evan believed that this one man could help him make better sense of the time that had already passed.

Chapter 17: The Arrival of Perry

"Hello there, Wise Walt!" Craig yelled out the same greeting to his grandfather that he did every time he saw him – it didn't matter when or where. He felt a particular kinship to the old man, and not just because they were a part of the same family. Craig could feel the sage wisdom oozing out of the pores of the older man every time he spoke, and Craig felt like he understood the words more acutely than others around him. Often, Walter would feel the same way.

As he ran up to his grandfather, Craig had a particular request on his mind. ""Hey, Wise Walt! I'd like you to tell me a special story today!"

"Oh, and what did you have in mind? Perhaps one of your favorites … how about the story of the giant, swaying towers?"

"No, no … I want something different! I want you to tell me a story about the most amazing person you have ever heard of!" Craig's eyes were ablaze; he wanted something truly enchanting.

"Well, let me think on that for just a moment." Walter rubbed his chin; the stubble on his beard was a little rough, but it seemed to be getting a little less gray with each passing day. After studying his thoughts very deeply, he suddenly looked up at the young man and a wry grin curled across his face, as his eyes began to sparkle.

"Yes, I think I know now" he said, confidently. "I'm going to tell you a story now of a man who came to this land many, many years ago. He was loved by many, but misunderstood by many more. In a lot of ways, he reminds me of you."

Craig sidled in closer. This was exactly what he wanted. He felt like he was able to understand the deeper meanings of Walter's stories much better than most anyone else around him, and he took particular pride in that fact. He convinced himself that he would drink in every detail of this story, and do his best to apply it to his own life – for he felt certain that some critical piece of knowledge might convey itself through history and land on him. Craig believed that people could actually plot their own course and effect change on those around them. He was a lot more like this particular character than he would ever know.

"It all began with the arrival of Perry" his grandfather began. "Perry King was a man who arrived in *Backstep* at about the same age your father did – he was about forty. But from the moment he arrived, he really shook up his world, and the people around him. It started the very moment he had the purple cloak wrapped around him."

"What happened? What happened?" Craig interrupted. He was so excited about the prospective plot of this story that he was losing a great deal of his patience. Walter understood this and did his best to calm the boy down, before continuing on.

"Well, while he was still asleep, as soon as the cloak was wrapped around him, he started humming the tune *Amazing Grace*. Gradually, others in the Field started picking up the tune and singing the words. By the time Perry woke up, it seems that the whole field had broken out into song. To this very day, the song remains one of our collective favorites. Before he got here, hardly anyone sang it; so, I guess you could say, he had an impact on *Backstep* before he had even opened his eyes for the first time."

This absolutely fascinated Craig. He wondered if he had made the same impact on people when he had first arrived; then, he suddenly snapped himself back to the details woven by the sage.

"After he opened his eyes and heard all the singing, he raised himself up and boldly cried out: 'I once had a dream about this … that, one day, all people would join in one voice and sing the words of that song … and now it has happened … it is a dream come true!' Then, he looked off to one side and saw the sun cresting beyond a purplish mountain. 'The mountaintop!' he exclaimed.

"But Walter, what significance does the mountaintop have to the story?" Craig demanded to know.

"Easy, easy; the story is far from over" Walter convinced him. "Perry was soon led to a hill, a short distance away, where he was to sit and listen to a sermon by one of the teachers. He was accompanied by a much older man named Jeremiah, who had just completed his own term as a teacher."

"It wasn't long after Perry had gotten himself comfortable on the ground in front of the teacher, then he started to interrupt the lesson with musings of his own. Sometimes, he would rant about the dreams he had and the 'progress that was to be made'; he didn't seem to understand that progress in the land of *Backstep* was contrary to the notions that came from the place he had been in previously. He was amazed that people of all colors were seated together, listening to the same message at the same time. Although he shook his head many times in disbelief, he tried to advise everyone that 'we still have far to go in order to bring freedom and equality to all people'."

Craig scratched his head. "Wait, I'm confused" he said. "Isn't this a place where everyone already is free and equal? And what do you think he meant by the statement 'we still have far to go'?"

"People had a very hard time understanding Perry, but he was a tremendous speaker" Walter indicated. "It has long been said that he had a presence that commanded attention and respect and that he had a deep baritone voice that could emit the most poetic language that the people had ever heard. From the very first day, he delivered passionate speeches – about equality, and about change; and although the people were captivated by his words, many of his so-called 'visions' had already come to fruition. Needless to say, if you preach about striving for things that are already firmly in place, people tend not to hang on to your words as much. Here, people want to be told stories of the past; they don't *want* to look toward the future."

"Why do people not want to look toward the future?" questioned Craig.

"My only guess is that because people already know how much time they have left here and they know when they will eventually depart, and they will be totally dependent on members of their families to see them through to the end of their journey, they give up a little of their independence. Perry could not understand why other people did not have the desire to be completely free and independent in their thoughts and in their actions; as long as he was committed to giving speeches, his message was pretty much in direct contradiction to the teachings of the rest of society."

"Did he get into trouble?" Craig asked.

"Well, not the kind of trouble that ever amounted to very much. Perry used to say that the world where he came from used to feature people being tortured and sacrificed simply because of the color of their skin. He wanted to make sure that would never happen again."

Craig studied these remarks. "I just can't comprehend a world in which people have to strive for progress, only to be held down by others. Here, everything just naturally progresses … isn't that the way it's supposed to be?"

"Indeed it is" responded the older man. "Every once in awhile, however, someone comes along to test the system". Walter's eyebrows furrowed when he said this, trying to peer deeply into the young man's soul. He then continued to speak:

"Perry was just that way – upon his arrival, he wanted to convince everyone that the order of *Backstep* was all wrong, and that people should fight to strive and move forward; to gain power and strength. The first few days, the sermons he delivered drew large crowds. But after awhile, like so many things here, people lost interest in him because he didn't really have a message that they understood. Around here, people become young and they gradually lose their cares, and they become more modest with the passing of time."

"After about a week, Perry lost all recollection of what he was initially trying to do when he first arrived. A great deal of his early tension was eased as he noticed family members and friends returning to be with him. They came from the same horrible place that he had come from; now, they were all sharing together in the glory and the magic of living peaceful lives, without any further mention of the color of their skin."

"With each passing day, he preached less and less, and by the time he had been in *Backstep* for two years, his preaching days were done. He became more active in the garden – in cultivating food for others. He worked as a gardener for the next twenty years. Perry was loved by many people, and would always make sure that people had enough food to eat. The man was transformed from 'Perry the Voice' to the 'King of the Garden'. To this day, if you ever hear a story about 'The King of the Garden', this is who they are really talking about."

"I guess I don't have to ask if the story for Perry ends 'happily ever after', because around here they all do – isn't that right?"

"It sure is! You know, it really is amazing to me that most everyone who first arrives here wants stories to end that way; then, after just a few days, it's naturally assumed that they will – so none of the storytellers even bother with that tag at the end anymore."

"What kind of childhood did Perry have? Did he do anything wonderful or spectacular?" Craig wanted to know.

"No, not really; by the time he began losing interest in growing things, he simply enjoyed playing games with other kids and listening to all the stories of the teachers. Some people in *Backstep* lamented the fact that he never was in a position to actually become a teacher ... but, as I have come to find out ..." (and here, Walter moved in a little closer and cautiously whispered the rest to his young colleague) – " ... you don't necessarily have to be older than eighty in order to teach!".

With that, Walter cast a furtive wink toward Craig, and the younger boy instantly grasped the meaning of the gesture and the story that had just been laid down before him.

"Thank you" Craig gratefully acknowledged. "I will try to apply the lessons I have learned from Perry to the rest of my life, as I get younger."

Walter smiled and shook his head. "As I have said many times before: Don't worry too much about the lessons you learn today; soon they will fade. You will re-learn things and forget about others ... it's all a part of the process. In the land I came from, there used to be an old phrase: 'You can't take it with you'. Just like when you first arrived here, you had nothing except for the family members who were here to greet you. Eventually, when you leave, you will have nothing except for the love of your family members who see you through to the end. Family to family; Perfection to perfection ... in the end, that's all that matters."

"Well then, why are we here, if we are not supposed to really accomplish anything?" Craig wondered aloud.

"But we *do* accomplish things; many, many great things" Walter assured him. "Much of what we do has a connection to the mending of old wounds, watching sicknesses and diseases eradicate themselves, and removing certain elements and imperfections from our systems and our society. Our land becomes a much better place, each and every day, albeit a little more simple and a little less 'driven'".

"Much of the change that occurs happens on a very small scale; things we aren't even aware of – they just seem to magically transform us into different people, little by little. Since my arrival, I have changed; since your arrival, just a short time ago, YOU have changed ... and as we change, it affects those things (and people) around us."

Craig thought for a moment. "I've noticed a real change in both my mom and dad" he said. "Mom, on the one hand, is happy but sometimes seems almost sad and withdrawn; dad, on the other hand, is so caught up in his work that I think he has time for little else, although he does his best to let us all know that we are loved and appreciated. I wish I knew what went on inside their heads."

"It's not worth worrying about" Walter said, as he put a calming hand on the young boy's shoulder. "You see, the worries that are on your mind today are some that you will only encounter a handful of times before they melt away. Some things will vanish instantly, as if they never even happened. For instance, you had an argument with your mother last week, over something small ... words were said, and you both went away angry.

"I can't even recall getting into an argument with her."

"That's my point, exactly" Walter said. "You are starting to grasp the concept and succumb to the will of this place ... it's easy to exert your own agenda, at least temporarily, but it takes a great deal of effort to hang onto things for any length of time."

"But ... can people actually hang on to things? Is it possible?" Craig questioned.

Walter rolled his eyes. He was torn between the notion of nudging the curious boy down a path filled with controversy or steering him in the direction of quiet complacency. He knew which way the elders would advise him to proceed. Knowing the young man well enough already, he decided to speak as openly and candidly as he knew how – he decided to let Craig make up his own mind.

"I've seen it happen. Eventually, as people get younger, even their best attempts to hang on to things lose focus, and they are inspired by or attracted to other things. This affects people who arrived here when they were old, like me, much more than people who are already in the prime of their youth – like you."

"I wouldn't really say that I am in my 'prime'" Craig replied. "I mean, look at me ... skinny, frail, sick with cancer; and I've - "

"-and you've still got your *whole life* ahead of you" Walter interrupted. "I don't expect you to understand the gift that you have been given, but you are going to get to witness the complete eradication of a sickness that killed many people in the land where you came from. The transformation has already started to happen; you have actually gotten stronger since your arrival, and you haven't been getting sick nearly as often. Eventually, the sickness will have removed itself from your body completely, and it will not ever survive in your memory bank."

"How come it is that you know so much?" Craig puzzled. "I mean, I have known that you were smart and all, but how is it that you are able to see both sides of the mirror – the past and the present?"

"I figured this question would come up eventually" Walter said as he began to nod his head and smile. "People like me … *really old* people like me … have their own unique set of gifts. They are physically weaker, but their minds are able to catch and hold onto things in a much different way from everyone else."

"If you will remember, all the teachers around here are very old; in fact, they have to be older than eighty years in order to be able to teach – because only those people have the expanded brain capacity to be able to think in both directions. They are truly the busiest people here – they are always telling stories, listening to others' dreams, processing information and making sense of things. They … we … are the ones who determine the basic structure of our civilization."

"So, are you trying to tell me that you guys control everything?" Craig challenged aloud.

"Well, it's not exactly like that. It's true, the rest of the people do rely on us very much; however, the way time passes takes its eventual toll on everyone; nothing ever stays the same. Progress reverts; though it may seem strange, progress is the very thing that gets in the way of perfection … if people ever became intensely driven to succeed in something or to gain power or influence, they would eventually realize that their efforts would be futile … because it all goes away after just seven days. That's all that history boils down to – seven days."

"I wonder if Perry tried to shake up things by making people believe that progress could actually be made and that people could get better at certain things, rather than simply sitting back and losing all their skills – and their intelligence."

"Well, there is often talk among the elders that he did just that", Walter nodded slowly, in affirmation.

"If he did such a thing, would people think he was dangerous?" Craig wondered.

Walter paused for a moment. Craig's questions were coming at him from every angle. Every answer that the older man posed only seemed to allow more questions to rise to the surface of the young boy's cauldron of insatiable curiosity.

"They may well have. But if he did, he was much more dangerous to himself than to anyone else."

"And why do you say that?" Craig wanted to know.

Walter just looked at his young companion and said with a smile "It's about time for me to go *do my thing* … but to try and answer your question, let me just say that once people understand that the purpose for being here is just working backward through the maze of their lives to reach the eventual perfection of the bright light, life comes down to simply enjoying the journey and one's own family. This may not seem like a suitable answer to you, but right now, it's about all I've got to give you."

As Walter got up and began gathering the few things that he needed to make his way toward his personal story-telling rock, Craig watched him closely. He wondered what it might be like to have the kind of mind that Walter had – to be able to think in both directions. He also thought about Perry, and wondered how dangerous of a man he actually could have become – a danger that would never be revealed in stories to the people.

Walking away, Walter waved to the young boy; consequently, he was thinking the very same thoughts. He only hoped that Craig would not become consumed with the notion that history could work in both directions. Walter's biggest fear was that the boy would make a valiant attempt to prove to himself and to everyone else that it could actually be done. Despite his best attempts at driving his thoughts toward positive energy, he suspected that Craig would somehow find trouble in this land of promised perfection.

Chapter 18: Something Seems Different

Every day, Mark and Evan came to work early. They went through their usual routine of drinking coffee, engaging in small talk, greeting all of the other doctors and orderlies as they came in, and perhaps reminiscing about some of the deliveries they had made over the past week – the only ones they could remember. After about an hour or so, one or the other of them would be summoned to one side of the field to meet up with the first families they would be dealing with. One particular day broke the mold – the only day of its kind that anyone could ever recall in the land of *Backstep*.

The day started out like most any other, with one exception: Mark was the first of the two to notice that the sky had an unusual greenish-yellow tinge to it, just before the sun came up to break the pallor. Neither one thought this to be an omen of any sort, and as the other doctors made their way in, Evan made a playful quip to his friend that he thought … "Perhaps today we will be busier than any day we can remember." Mark and the other doctors simply brushed it off as they prepared for the upcoming workload. None of them seemed really surprised when no one showed up at the field after the first hour; but after the second hour had passed and there were still no arrivals, they began to become a little confused.

By the time the sun had positioned itself directly overhead, the normally warm and inviting orb hid itself behind the clouds; it was almost as if it did not want to witness the strange happenings taking place far below. The empty field seemed sad; usually, it was bustling with activity, as families welcomed new members and happy tears were shed all around. Mark scratched his head as he and the others looked all around, surveying the surroundings. Serving as the mouthpiece for the crowd, he suddenly blurted out (to no one in particular) the question they were all thinking:

"Why hasn't anyone come yet? What does all this silence mean?"

Evan came up next to him and laid a hand on his friend's shoulder. His words were delivered calmly, but with a great deal of clarity and purpose:

"Craig told me there might be days like these, every once in awhile. He told me that in his dreams, sometimes, there are periods where silence is everywhere – periods of silence that are so prolonged that the quiet is almost deafening. He said that these are the moments when we most question and doubt ourselves, and we begin to de-value our own sense of purpose and worth to the world around us. He also said that these are good opportunities for us to reflect upon our families and other loved ones, and to simply appreciate what we have and what we know, rather than to become filled with fear and reservations over things we may never know."

Mark's bottom jaw dropped. He knew that Craig was an intelligent boy, but this was almost beyond any stream of consciousness he could imagine, and he was absolutely stunned; so much so that he didn't know how to respond, at first. As he grappled for words, Evan provided his own brand of reassurance.

"Craig is so complex. For a boy so young, ravaged by cancer and yet brimming with hope and optimism, it's hard sometimes for me to fully appreciate the wisdom of his words. It's funny, but it's almost like having a teacher living under my own roof. He makes a lot of sense, but I know that his intelligence and perception of this place far exceeds those around him – even some of the elders."

"*Especially* the elders" Mark said, passionately. "Don't you worry sometimes that he says too much; that perhaps some of his 'ideas' won't be readily accepted by the governing body, thus making him somewhat dangerous to the status quo?"

"I worried for the first couple of days" Evan admitted. "But once he started working with the kids at the hospital and converted most of his priorities toward caring for and providing a brighter outlook for all those kids, most of my worry seemed to melt away. He does talk to me a lot at night, before bedtime, however."

"Oh, and what kind of things do you talk about?" Mark curiously pondered.

"Mostly, it's him talking and me listening. It's not so much the perspective I provide as his elder; instead, I am simply a sounding board and a loving and caring parent. I mean, we spend so much time here in the field and then with the families at our nightly dinners that it's hard to have any other quality time with him, except at the end of the day."

Mark smiled; however, it didn't seem happy, but rather forced. "I'd still like to know where he comes up with these ideas or 'notions', as he calls them."

Evan continued to try and rationalize to his colleague. "Craig and Walter have been spending a lot of time together during the day. I don't want to say outright that Craig is getting his wisdom directly from Walter, and it does worry me sometimes that a boy should be spending so much time with an elder, instead of playing with other kids closer to his own age."

"Have you thought of the possibility that it's just a kid enjoying some quality time with his grandfather?" Mark asked.

"I've thought about that" Evan responded. "But I have also thought of the possibility that Walter could be getting some of *his* wisdom from a twelve year-old!"

The two men looked at each other and suddenly they both broke up into laughter; it really helped to ease the tension that had been building. As they chuckled, two of the other doctors came over to join them.

"I'm certainly glad to see you two yucking it up, because this inactivity is driving me nuts!" said David, who had drifted over more out of boredom than anything else. He and Justin were growing just as impatient as everyone around them, and they all hoped they would not get into an argument over the first client of the day. Little did they know that their collective wait would indeed be a long one!

After an interminable period of silence and waiting, they all noticed a lone figure making his way to the north edge of the field. Among them, they wondered who might be the recipient of the day's first case. Before anyone else could move, however, Evan had already begun to make his way over. He knew the face; this time, he had remembered, because he had seen this same face every day for the past week. Ever since the last time the man known simply as Whitehouse had foretold of the last delivery, Evan had paid close attention to him, from a distance. As he looked around, though, Evan became more and more uneasy; he was almost at the meet-up point when he realized that there was no one else around – no family, no friends … no large gathering, which usually coincided with this man's appearances.

Evan was obviously perplexed by this strange twist. Whitehouse sensed this and leaned in slowly; in a whisper, he delivered what would turn out to be his final words to the doctor:

"There is no family today; there is no delivery today. But believe me when I tell you that there will be one tomorrow, and it will be accompanied by one of the largest throngs you have ever witnessed. I will no longer make visits to the East Field; if you ever see me again, you will not know me and you will not recall any of the events that brought me here. Tomorrow, my final burden will be released and I will be a free man – free to live out the rest of my days in relative peace and happiness … goodbye."

With no more fanfare than that, Whitehouse turned and walked away. Evan studied his walk, trying to pick up any clue that he could from the man's gait, but he failed to gain any access to the man's soul from what he observed. Eventually, he accepted the knowledge that had been imparted, and tried to let go of the rest.

Upon returning to the others, Mark offered his thoughts. "I've seen that guy around here before … what did he want?"

Evan tried to cover-up what he knew and tried to deny the rest of what he suspected – that the man, Whitehouse, must somehow be involved in the life of one of the next day's new arrivals.

"Oh nothing; he just wanted to tell me something he remembered from the last time we met."

It was a very clever lie, but Mark bought it, as did the others who were eavesdropping. Proud of himself for the ruse he had created on-the-fly, Evan turned to get one final glimpse of the man who foretold arrivals, but he had already vanished from sight. All that he knew conflicted with what he believed. How could Whitehouse be sure that the two paths would never cross again, and that there would be no recollection on the part of either man if they should, by chance, happen to meet beyond this day?

Whitehouse felt a huge burden lifted from his breast, but he knew that although some peace would come to him soon, true happiness for him was many years down the road; tomorrow was just the next large reverse step in the entire process. The thing that he could not tell anyone, not even the doctor he had entrusted, was that (in a previous life) he had been responsible for many deaths – he was, in actuality, a reformed killing machine. In the world where he came from, he had tortured, brutalized and murdered several children — all as a result of a blind rage toward his own father, who had abused him when he was younger.

Before he had even arrived at *Backstep*, he had accepted an invitation to walk a backwards journey, to help undo some of the nightmares that he had single-handedly perpetuated on numerous families, and to walk into a family that would love him in a way that he had never known before. Right now, he still felt a little empty inside, but he was relieved to know that he was now moving in a much better direction. His premonitions told him that it was important to be here at the field for each and every delivery so that he could truly see love in the expressions of the families; he was reminded about how much his own mother loved him when he had arrived in this land. Whitehouse was amazed how, in such a short span of time, he had been able to effectively set aside feelings of rage. His sense of power and domination had melted away, and he simply wanted to be near his own mother.

None of the other family members knew of his problems, except for his mother; and she would say nothing, because she kept clinging to the hope and belief that things would only get better for her and for her son. So far, that belief was paying more dividends than she could have ever imagined. Her family was truly coming together; Sarah knew that, one day, she would carry her baby, Craig, in her arms and deposit him in the nest that would transport him away to the bright light of perfection. She also knew that many years would pass before that would actually happen, and she felt very fortunate to be able to spend as much time with him as she wanted, in the meantime. Eventually, Craig's father would also return; she hoped that their new life together would be much different from the old life. Every night, she said a prayer to that effect.

By the time Whitehouse departed, Mark and Evan began to realize that maybe the oddest circumstance of all had befallen them: there might not be any deliveries that day! Mark had been told that this had happened one other time in recorded *Backstep* history, but none who had ever heard the story actually believed it, because it had happened such a long time before. The other reason why people tended to be incredulous about the legend was simply due to the fact that it upset the nice, neat, quiet routine that so many had become accustomed to and allowed them to relax and ease into their own lives and families. There were not too many things that caused a great deal of shock or angst among the citizens — and even if they did, they would fade from view relatively quickly.

Evan tried to piece together the events of previous deliveries that involved the appearance of this man Whitehouse. He tried his best to make some kind of mental connection – what was it that linked this man with all these young children of other families? He was thoroughly confused – he didn't know whether to view this man Craig as a divine presence or an evil force from another world.

The doctors continued in their idle discussions with one another, as they each grabbed another cup of coffee. This break in the activity provided them with a unique opportunity to converse with each other – to laugh, joke, and reminisce – things that they were able to do only sporadically at their evening dinners; it was different, however, to be afforded the chance to do this at work, apart from their own families. This gathering also included the orderlies, none of whom were included in those special nightly banquets anyway; so, in a way, it was almost as if some benevolent hand had swept across the field and allowed this group of busy people to share their own family moment, both special and unique - perhaps for the only time in their lives.

The time passed and everyone working in the field lost track because they were caught up in the sharing of these moments with their "work family". Finally, one of the underlings noticed that the sun was beginning to dip.

"It's almost time to go home!" she announced.

"And not one single delivery … can you imagine that!" echoed one of the doctors. Vivian had really been struggling – her cancer was really eating away at her ability to do good work. This period of inactivity gave her a much-needed rest and enabled her to cleverly hide the exhaustion and frustration that she felt. Every time she looked over toward Evan, she felt both downtrodden and a tad bit angry – neither of these emotions were things that she either understood or liked … she just hoped they would go away. For now, she was just happy enough that her own physical condition would not stand in the way of all the daily work that was carried on in the field; at least today, anyway. She clung tight to the promise that her days would become more rich and vibrant and free of pain, and she hoped those days were not too far away.

It is always amazing how periods of quiet can allow one to focus internally, and to open up the can of worry within the mind that lays buried deep in the soul, under layers of activity and "business-as-usual". Evan's mind was working on three different puzzles at once. The first of these puzzles was the man who had just left him. No matter how hard he tried, he could not figure out the complexities of Whitehouse – what brought him there, what his connections to all the children might be, and what went on inside his head. No one else seemed to know him, and no one else seemed to be the least bit interested in his story. There was only one person in the field that Whitehouse had any impact on – and although Evan felt that impact in a strong way, its overall significance seemed lost in darkness.

The other puzzle that Evan was working on was his son: the more he thought about it, the more concerned he became that his own Craig was somehow different from every other soul in the world. Some of the words that Mark had said to him earlier hit home once again, and he began to worry that perhaps some people might view Craig as some sort of lunatic because of some of the strange ideas he espoused. Or, he feared, people might see him as "damaged goods" because of the cancer, and keep their kids away from him. One of Craig's gifts had clearly emerged, and it was something that few people even came close to understanding. Evan felt that this could pose some sort of danger to him and his family, although he couldn't pinpoint exactly what they might be. He just brushed these thoughts away, and returned his mindset to his own set of daily rituals and practices. He decided not to let a host of *unknowns* ruin his day.

Finally, his thoughts turned to Addy, the one person who had been his constant beacon of light throughout his time in *Backstep*. He had noticed that she was appearing more and more withdrawn – the same realization had occurred to Craig, although the two of them never mentioned it during their nightly chats. He wasn't necessarily worried about Addy; however, he sensed that she was carrying around some kind of burden – sandwiched among the layers of her otherwise happy life. He wanted to find out what the deep dark secret might be, but he hesitated to probe too much. Walter had told him, time and again, that there were simply some things that people should not get involved in, even if their curiosities happened to be piqued – those notions would eventually depart and cause no further concern.

After a short while, Evan decided to leave the three puzzles alone, and he began packing up his things so that he could join his family at the nightly banquet. For a brief moment, he wondered what might happen down the road, when there would be no feast for him to partake in. It was a thought that only was allowed to exist for a fleeting moment; he quickly brushed it aside and hurried home to gather the rest of his family.

Evan reflected on the fact that his life was a good one: there were things he believed in, things he understood, and people whom he loved and who loved him in return. The nightmares that had plagued him when he had first arrived were gone now; they had been replaced by dreams of a happy family ... and each family member was getting younger and happier, by the day ... What could possibly be better than that?

Chapter 19: The Council

Walter received a note to attend a special session of the Council that was to meet later that evening. He didn't know exactly what the topic would be, but he was afraid that it would center on Craig. Lately, the young boy had begun spouting off strange ideas about "change" and "progress" – some of the elders knew that Walter had told him the story of Perry King and Walter was now concerned that the young boy had taken to heart some of the heretical sayings and proposed "teachings" of the much-beloved yet misunderstood young sage from the past.

Noticing the piece of paper that Walter was trying to keep out of sight, Margaret became a little curious.

"What is this all about, dear?" she wanted to know.

Walter studied the notice again and rubbed the side of his face. "I'm not exactly sure what this is about" he offered. "It may have something to do with the fact that I haven't got a whole lot of teaching time left ... or, then again, it could be-"

"Craig." Margaret blurted out the name before she could control herself. She had also noticed how the boy had changed slightly – as his bones grew stronger and he became more and more steady on his feet, his words were becoming bolder as well. Not many of the adults cared so much; but the children, particularly the ones in the hospital, were very much under his influence. This was becoming a source of concern for the elders – there was much murmuring, away from the general population. Walter had shared some of the details when he returned from his nightly meetings with the Council, but this – THIS was a special session. She was both intrigued and worried for her partner at the same time.

The old man read the look of anxiety on her face. He walked over and placed his hands on top of hers.

"There, there; it's going to be all right. I'm sure it's nothing – probably just some old boring business to tend to."

"I'm sure you're right" Margaret hesitantly agreed; but despite the fact that they were trying to re-assure themselves and each other, they were both living a lie at that moment. They knew that Craig was busy with the other children at the hospital at that same time, and during the course of their fun and games it was a perfect opportunity for him to launch into his propaganda: the idea that people can cause change, and alter the course of history, as opposed to the natural progression already laid out for the people of *Backstep*.

"Doesn't Craig know that people just follow the natural inclinations of their hearts and stick with their families?" Doesn't he realize that is the only way to work toward perfection?"

Walter thought about Margaret's questions and then he said something quite prophetic:

"Maybe he doesn't want perfection … maybe he feels like we're not supposed to end up perfect; that we just live our own independent lives until we burn up like a comet in the sky or an ember on the fire."

"I don't want to believe that he thinks like that … and I don't want to believe those things that some of the other elders are saying about him."

"So, you've heard?" Walter asked his partner.

"Of course I have! I don't just sit around all day with blind eyes and deaf ears! I know what's going on … and I have a pretty good idea that when you go to that meeting tonight they are going to take you to task, to see about reigning-in that young man, and get him to start talking and acting the way the elders have prescribed."

"But Margaret – he is only a child! Every day, he becomes younger and filled with innocence; things don't build up layer upon layer as they did in the old world. I will do my best to convince them that he poses no harm or threat to our society and that they all should just leave it alone."

"They are probably all afraid – I'm sure they've never dealt with anything like this before" she convincingly argued.

"Well, it's probably my fault that I let the story of Perry slip out – it may have filled him with ideas."

Margaret began to raise her voice. "You knew *exactly* what you were doing, didn't you? Of all the stories you could have told him, you had to bring up the one about the bold character who walked his own walk, against the grain of many in his own world, and who was labeled as both a hero and a heretic."

"I thought he should at least know about King, because the two of them are very much alike" Walter said, as he cautiously tried to back out of a confrontation with the now-steaming woman.

"Well, at least time took its toll and eventually brought him back in line – that's how it works" Margaret sighed with a bit of relief. "I just hope Craig doesn't go through a lot of short-term pain before he loses this little 'cause' he is trying to be the champion of."

"I think our young man has endured enough pain since he arrived" Walter rationalized. "The way I see it, he will never be more brash and bold than he is right now. He is getting stronger, that's true – but he is also becoming more childlike with each passing day ... even his questions to me the last few days have seemed rather juvenile."

Margaret was puzzled. "What exactly is it, do you think, that Craig is asking the other children to do? Why is he, all of a sudden, so dangerous?"

"My guess is" Walter began, "that he is trying to lead the children to a sense of independence. Right now, many of them feel a sense of loneliness with the cancer that has taken hold of their bodies – and there is nothing their parents can do about it. Craig tells them to believe in themselves and to have faith in themselves – as the cancer goes away, the kids feel more confident and believe that they were the ones who drove their own cancer into oblivion – that it had little to do with the love and support of their own families. The elders are concerned that Craig is threatening the basic structure of the family, by making kids think they don't need their parents."

"But that's ridiculous!" Margaret swatted the air with her hand and stomped her foot.

"ALL CHILDREN, at some point, rebel against their own parents; it's only natural. Time eventually brings them around and they realize that they have to rely on parents more and more, not less and less. No matter how much people may try to fight against this force, they cannot overcome it."

"You're right, my dear; so, in essence, this will be a lot like a test."

"Aha! So you tricked him into all this, isn't that right?" she challenged. "It's come down to you laying out a challenge for your own grandson."

"You may think so, but I'm not just challenging him" Walter confided. "This is also a test for me!"

The East Field started out quiet, as the doctors made their way in once again. After having just finished a day with not one single delivery, they all wondered what this day might have in store for them. At least one of the doctors, however, knew pretty much what to expect.

Evan knew he would not see Whitehouse at all, but he felt the man's presence with every step he took in the field. At some point, he knew that a crowd would be gathering; and from what the man had told him, it would be a massive crowd indeed. As he began his first case, he once again became absorbed in his routine and he did not notice, right off, the group of fourteen people that had congregated on the east side of the field. He first acknowledged what was going on as the crowd grew to about twenty-five; by the time he had finished his second delivery, the throng numbered over one hundred. None of the other doctors ventured anywhere near this group – they all knew this was Evan's territory and they respectfully acquiesced.

When the time beckoned him, the doctor made his way over to the gathering mass. As he neared the edge of the field, the crowd parted and a man and woman emerged, holding hands. Their eyes looked red and puffy, and they seemed exhausted; but rather than sadness, what he saw in their faces was great anticipation; great hopefulness. It was a look he had seen many times before, but this time felt much different from anything he remembered. Evan felt the deep presence of Whitehouse surrounding them, although he knew that the man with that name was nowhere around.

He went through his set of instructions to the young couple and completed the delivery as nonchalantly as ever. When the young girl, Rema, was finally brought into the world, Evan felt a huge wave of relief and euphoria – unlike any he had ever felt. It never ceased to amaze him how so many people would always be so intrigued with the arrival of a young child, though it happened on a somewhat regular basis. He also knew that not all of the children who came in at a young age were victims, at one time, of a disease that would have to be reversed and then eradicated. Some of these children had chilling, dark stories that coincided with their arrival. Many would be drastically altered, in time, by the storytellers, but he knew that would have to wait until the children actually had the chance to confront their own dreams and present them to the Council.

Evan wondered what kind of story Rema had; what exactly was the event that brought her to this place? He could only imagine how the parents must have waited and pined for their daughter and what kind of life they led, previous to this momentous occasion. Evan also knew that Rema's coming meant that the "happily ever after" part of her life could now unfold – whatever happened before now would eventually fade, and there would be nothing but happy days ahead.

A cool breeze brushed past Evan as he stood there surveying the situation; suddenly, it occurred to him that – somewhere – the same light wind was probably passing over the man who would no longer pay visits to the field. Just then, it dawned on Evan that Whitehouse was the cause of all this; he was the one responsible for the horrible disappearances of young children in another world – another lifetime. But unlike the overriding sense of gloom and fear that cast a pall of ominous shadows over those events, these were painted in happiness – love reunited. It was such an awesome thing to feel, and to witness.

He continued to watch as the man and woman sprawled across the young girl, weeping joyously. The crowd dispersed, little by little, until only one person stood there. Evan blinked his eyes hard, because he couldn't believe who it was. The face was the same one that greeted him in the morning and the last one he saw every night, before the hands of time made their dramatic leap backward … it was Addy!

Stunned, Evan made his way back over to where she stood; now, he was joined by Mark. Before he could ask the question himself, Mark beat him to the point.

"What are you doing here?" Mark wanted to know.

"Yes, I'd like to know the same thing" Evan echoed.

Addy stood silently for a moment, then looked down, away from both of them. "As a mother, I can relate to having a sense of loss for a long time, then having it filled again" she said. "Actually, I know the mother quite well; her name is Ivanna. The two of us, along with several other ladies, gather at the park every day to talk and to watch the children play. For a long time, she has watched her other daughter play, but the last few days have seemed really empty for her; before today, I never knew why. This morning, some strange calling drew me to the field, to be here … I guess, to be with her. Tomorrow, she will be a completely different person; just like I was when Craig arrived."

Mark and Evan looked at each other, quite puzzled. Evan posed the question that was on Mark's mind as well:

"How did you know to come down here at the exact time that you did?"

Addy looked up into Evan's eyes. "I know you may not believe this, but I was told to come here today during my dream last night."

"So, why didn't you say anything about it this morning?"

"I was told not to."

The doctor shrugged, because he knew there were many mysteries of life and dreams that he just couldn't understand. He had a wife who kept things hidden from him, a son who was boldly eccentric and recovering from a debilitating disease, and a father who was one of the wisest men in all the land; and yet, here he was – the one who was truly performing miracles – bringing life to entire families – why didn't he feel like he was something special?

Mark seemed to detect that Evan was throwing himself a little pity party; he could always read people's expressions very well. Clapping his colleague on the back, he did what he could to bolster both his confidence and his ego. What seemed, at first, like just another routine procedure, was now turning out to be much more life-altering.

"Just let it go, my friend ... Addy, we'll see you tonight." With those words, he turned the doctor around and, with his arm firmly gripping Evan's shoulder, forced him away. He looked back toward his sister and gave her a nod, indicating that things would be all right and that she should not worry any further. She gave him a smile, blew him a kiss and mouthed the words "Thank You", before turning to leave the field, which was full of activity, by that time.

As the two men walked to the center of the field, dodging other doctors along the way, Evan commented (to no one in particular):

"I just wish she would tell me things!"

Mark considered the statement and chose his next words thoughtfully.

"I'm sure if there was anything you really needed to know, she would tell you" he assured his friend.

. "Think about it: we all have our little secrets ... I'm sure there are a few things buried deep within that old soul of yours that you haven't shared with her."

"Not really" Evan fired back. "My life is pretty much an open book; and besides, she's been here a lot longer than I have!"

"When you consider the fact that our memories only go back seven days, none of us has really been here too much longer than anybody else ... except, of course, for the *really* old people!"

With that, Evan let out a snort, in suppressed laughter. Mark was always good about making other people feel at ease. Soon, they would be immersed in their work once again; in just seven days, all knowledge of this series of children who had appeared over the past week would be erased from their memories – the only thing that would remain would be the children themselves and the legends that would be woven by others – who would tell of the miracles and ordinary occurrences built-in to the rest of their lives.

As the day ended and the sun dipped, the doctors and their families gathered once again for their traditional feast. Nothing would be any different tonight; however, Evan could not get Whitehouse out of his mind. Good, bad, or otherwise, he found that the man had woven himself into the fabric of his life, and it would be hard to shake. Already, he was beginning to forget what the man looked like; he knew that if he didn't see him again in the next day or so, after awhile he would simply be another anonymous face passing in the middle of a crowd. But, for now, his mind was picking furiously at the details of Whitehouse's interaction with him at the field.

"What's the matter dear? You seem a little preoccupied." Addy wanted to know what was bothering her mate.

"Oh, it's nothing, really." Evan brushed her off, rather callously; then, a bolt of realization came crashing down upon him – the very thing he had accused Addy of doing was the same thing he was doing now … keeping something hidden, and blocking out his family! He grabbed both of her hands and looked into her face.

"I'm sorry" he said. "I didn't mean to treat you like that. You and Craig are the two most important things in the world to me, and I'm sure I haven't told you enough about things going on in my life. Sometimes, I worry that I might bore you or talk about things that you have either absolutely no interest in or no connection to."

A tear formed in her eye; but it was a happy little tear. "But we're family" she uttered. "Whatever affects you, also affects me."

"It works both ways, you know" he winked.

"Yes, I know." She kissed him on the cheek and they resumed their dinner, with the ever-gregarious Craig at their side. For now, their lives would carry on in the usual way.

Meanwhile, on the other side of the village, old men and women, bearing torches, made their way silently to a large cave. This was no Council of Dreams – this was a special session; and although he wasn't

F. *Thomas Jones*

told outright, Walter knew that he would soon be the center of attention, and he didn't like it one bit.

"All of this because of one little boy" he thought. Then, his attention suddenly shifted. He began to toy with a new course of action.

"What would *he* do?" Walter asked himself. "In this situation, what would Craig do?"

Chapter 20: A Soulful Confession

In the old world, sometimes gloomy weather would provide the backdrop for dismal events. *Backstep* was different; every day was filled with both sun and clouds. There was new promise and new hope, because life just got a little more perfect for each and every one of its inhabitants … all, that is, except for some of the elders.

When the Council meeting finally dispersed, they all had come to agreement about how to handle Craig; it was actually a much better outcome than Walter had anticipated. Under the new arrangement, Walter would continue to teach until his days as an instructor came to an end, which was not too far off. Then, he would continue with the new job he had been assigned – as a personal mentor to his grandson. The Council realized the close bond that existed between the two, and they wanted to be able to take advantage of that so they could keep a close eye on the youngster and be well apprised of all his activities. At first, Walter almost felt like he was being made into a spy; but the fact that his new "job" would be something he would probably do anyway, as a natural consequence, made him much more comfortable. He wondered how long this might last, before Craig finally fell into simply being a kid.

Under the arrangement, Walter would have to report in to the elders every evening, while Craig had dinner with his family. He would then be given new instructions about which teachers to take Craig to the next day. Since the teachers had all their respective scripts and stories mapped out, it was easy enough for them to manipulate Craig's instruction – they could just simply choose the particular stories that they wanted him to hear, in a specified order, and they could do their best to control his thoughts and stream of consciousness. Walter would then be able to report how these stories were received and what, if any, reaction the young boy had. At first, Walter buckled at the great lengths the elders would go to control and manipulate a twelve year-old, but he understood that if the Council determined this to be something in the family's best interest, he should go along with it. He did bristle a little when the Council announced its decision that the story of Perry King was being banished from the list of accepted teachings.

For the most part, Walter was unencumbered as far as his own storytelling was concerned; he could continue to choose the stories that he liked the most – the ones that he felt were the most entertaining to the children. As long as Craig was at the hospital, he didn't have to worry too much; there were a couple of elders there who would keep an eye on things for awhile, at least. At some point, Walter would take over as the new guardian of the boy's daily activities, and the people assigned by the Council to watch Craig would no longer be necessary.

After another wonderful meal and several rounds of emotional and grateful accolades from other families, Evan and his own little family returned to their home. Evan and Addy noticed that Craig was filled with energy; more so than usual. He constantly talked about children at the hospital, games they had played, and stories he had told them. The parents were amazed at how well he could commit to memory the things he heard from the elders during his afternoon lessons, and weave them into stories of his own to tell the children in the morning. The elders made sure that he didn't take too many liberties with the stories – if he did, the exposed children would simply have to be "re-programmed".

Two women at the hospital oversaw things and reported back to the Council. They didn't mind their assignment – in part, because they knew it was only for a short period of time; but also because they were intrigued by the wisdom and energy that such a young lad could possess. Like so many others, they were amazed and had to fight off falling under his spell of infectious positive determination.

Craig didn't just wind down gradually at the end of the day – he went full speed, and then simply dropped into a fast sleep when his dreams beckoned him; and he always slept with a smile on his face. Tonight was no different. The two parents watched as the boy drifted into a land of dreams that only he would be able to understand and interpret – something that both bothered them and fascinated them at the same time.

As they looked on during his state of peacefulness, Addy suddenly reached for and grabbed both of Evan's hands. "I haven't been completely open with you" she said. "I've got something we need to talk about."

Evan looked into her eyes. He had hoped this moment would come. For days, he had worried that she was keeping some painful secret from him that might alter their relationship in some way. He had no idea what it might be, but he looked forward to knowing exactly what it was.

"I detected something was wrong" he said. "I could see it in your eyes."

"Yes, the eyes always give it away" she sheepishly responded. "I do my best to keep things hidden sometimes; not because I want to, but because there is nothing anyone can do about this particular situation."

She gripped his hands tightly, then continued. "I have another daughter" she announced. "It is a thread of a life that is not connected to you, and it will only be re-connected with me years down the road – after you and I are no longer together."

Evan allowed her words to soak in; this was certainly something he had not expected. Very carefully, he thought about how he should respond – what his proper course of action should be; but he was dumbfounded.

Addy misread his thoughts, thinking he was becoming angry with her. "Don't be mad!" she pleaded. "I have been faithful to you and will continue to be, until we are both too young for this kind of relationship anymore."

"I'm not mad" Evan said, as the expression on his face softened. "I'm just trying to figure out how you know you have a daughter, yet you have never mentioned her before. How do you even know that she exists? Have you seen her?"

The mother of two then went on to reveal to Evan what she knew, how she felt, and what she had been guided to do in her life. She told him of the daily visits to the park: how she watched the young lady playing, committing her features and mannerisms to memory each and every day so that she would not forget. Addy knew that it would be wrong to reveal herself to Diana or to the loving couple to whom she belonged as a part of their family; she knew that eventually the two of them would come together, in the right way, at the right time. In the meantime, however, Addy believed it was her daily duty to observe from a distance – to maintain the bond between them – silently.

She didn't know how long she had been doing this; for all she knew, it was all her life. When the mind only allows you to hold onto things for seven days, you must really develop a steady routine in order to be able to maintain anything long-term; Addy knew that. Her dreams told her where to go so that the bond would not be severed; her dreams were her constant guide and companion.

Her dreams told her other things too, sometimes – and showed her things that she didn't always recognize or understand. Occasionally, she saw visions of a very old woman being pulled up out of the ground; this woman was by herself, except for one other person – a handsome, middle-aged woman who held the older, frail one in her arms and rocked her like a little baby. In this vision, no words were ever spoken; there were only tears and smiles, and the blissful humming of a tune that she knew very well. What Addy did *not* remember was the fact that this actually did happen – the older woman in the vision was her, upon her arrival to *Backstep*. And the person who was there to greet her, to help bring her into the world, was Diana!

Diana had been called to the field on that day, many, many years before, to help care for an old woman who would go on to become a much-loved teacher for twelve years, and then continue on to a life of value, although her days would be somewhat hollow in many ways. Diana, a mother herself, would continue her life in reverse – she would provide the loving support for her adoptive parents, once harvested; she would know the joy of witnessing the achievement of perfection for her own two children. She would then continue to grow younger, losing her cares and inhibitions, and grow closer toward perfection herself … a long life, with no recollection of anything beyond seven days. In that regard, she and Addy were very much alike.

When Addy had finished telling Evan the extent of what she knew and felt, she collapsed into his arms and wept like never before. Her tears were not bitter; they were a relief. Although she knew that this was not a topic they would openly discuss, particularly around Craig, she was a little more at ease with herself for shedding the burden. Addy would continue her daily monitoring of Diana; eventually, Evan would forget all about it, and it would once again become just a part of Addy's world – a part that she would not have to keep hidden from her partner any longer. She could at least tell him where she was going, but wouldn't have to keep the reason veiled in secrecy or shame. In that very moment of soulful confession, Addy became much more confident and assured that what she was doing was indeed the right thing; and she began to look even more forward to the future, and her life as an even younger woman – and mother to Diana.

Evan and Addy both slept well that night-- and although their dreams took them along different paths, they were both content; one knowing that a huge burden had been lifted, while the other was relieved in knowing that nothing was being kept hidden from him by his loving partner. Secrets can be revealed, fade, then be revealed again – only to fade again; but the bond among family members is something that lasts ... beyond all measures of time. The lesson of *family* is no doubt the most important one that the inhabitants of *Backstep* come to realize ... just as Addy and Evan did on that special night.

The next day, Evan awoke rested and refreshed. He was revitalized, more so than usual. For some reason, he felt like he had just conquered the world, though he knew he was now in a world that could simply not be conquered. Addy, having gotten up shortly after her mate, felt quite the same way – for her, however, it was like reaching the summit of the highest mountain, after a long climb – exhilarating and exhausting, all at once.

As she busily prepared breakfast, Evan waited until Craig was out of earshot and then he asked the question:

"Are you going to see her today?"

"I go to see her *every* day" she replied. "But I'm happy today for another reason; I'm happy today for Ivanna Jensen."

"Oh yes, I remember the name. She was the lady yesterday – with the young girl, right?"

"Yes. For quite some time, she has been at the park with me and several others who gather to watch the children playing. She has another daughter too, but there was always something missing. Now, I know what that something was."

"Rema!" Craig yelled from the opposite end of the room.

"How in the world did he hear us?" Evan whispered.

"I don't know; I guess he just – THAT'S RIGHT DEAR, REMA!" Addy tried to deflect her son's attention away from their conversation, but she was also intrigued how the boy knew. She started to become flustered; then, Craig walked over with a big smile on his face and looked up into her eyes.

"That's okay; you're my star!" he announced in dramatic fashion, with his arms spread wide, as he came in for a hug. Addy threw her arms around him and looked over his shoulder toward Evan. She seemed to shrug as if resigned to the fact that she was no longer in charge of the conversation. Evan nodded, blew her a kiss, slapped Craig on the rump, and headed out the door.

After cleaning up, mother and son made their daily visit to the hospital.

All the youngsters greeted him in the usual way. Today, there was one new kid in the intensive care unit – a little boy who had not been there the day before. Craig made it a point to drop in on this newcomer and spend some time with him, before he did anything else. The boy's name was Derrick Hiatt. Craig's father had not mentioned that another boy, stricken with cancer, had been harvested the day before; but it didn't matter, because Craig already knew … he ALWAYS knew. The boy was a little older than Craig, but the pale features and ravaged body made Derrick look much older than he actually was.

Craig sat down on the edge of the bed and began to smooth down the covers with his hand. "Hi" he said, softly and politely. "My name is Craig."

The older boy opened one eye and studied him for a moment, which seemed like an eternity. In a strained voice, he was able to force out just a few words:

"Oh yeah … you must be the one that my parents told me about … you're the 'Miracle Man', right?"

"Well, some people call me that" he said, in a blush; "but the truth of the matter is, what's inside of YOU is the true miracle!" He then began to tell Derrick about all the hope and promise of this new and wonderful life and of all the things that he would be able to do and to accomplish, after just a brief stay in the ICU. He told the boy how he had been very sick himself, upon his arrival, and how he had gotten better and stronger every day, simply by believing in himself.

The sick boy was incredulous at first, and in a great deal of physical pain; however, Craig continued to talk with him for a few more minutes. When he was ready to leave, Craig bent down next to Derrick's ear and whispered something that no one else could hear. Almost instantly, Derrick fell asleep and a relaxed smile spread out across his face, as he slumbered.

Two very interested onlookers witnessed the whole thing and they studied it intently. The two women, assigned to monitor Craig's activities, looked at each other in bewilderment. Finally, one said to the other:

"What do you think he said?"

"Does it really matter? Look at the expression on that boy's face; look how peacefully he is resting. Whatever Craig did or said, it seems to have made a huge difference in the quality of life for this particular young man."

The other woman nodded her head in agreement. "You know, maybe the members of the Council are wrong. It could very well be that Craig is not a danger at all, but rather more like a prophet."

Whether he had planned it or not, the young lion had just gained two more converts; it was the very thing that certain members of the Council worried about. The more people that they brought in to shadow Craig, the more it seemed really liked him – to the point where some of the elders really felt threatened.

In the meeting the night before, one of them asked the question: "What would happen to our society if the people chose a new leader – a twelve year-old?" The Council members tried to rationalize among themselves that putting a youngster in charge would create mass chaos – day by day, the child would become less and less interested in the well-being of all and simply be concerned with his own selfish whims. If the people saw that and emulated that same behavior, *Backstep* would forever be altered and the promise of perfection would be shattered for almost everyone.

Despite this fear, there was evidence – each and every day – that what Craig was doing was indeed good: he brought smiles to the faces of those who were in pain, hope to those families in need of some; and he was transforming gloom into laughter. Everything he touched seemed to brighten; now he simply had to work on the somewhat fearful and misguided hearts of the men and women in charge.

When Addy arrived at the park, Ivanna was already there with her two daughters. Rema looked completely normal. She and her younger sister Krissy ran and laughed as if the two had never been separated. It seemed odd to Addy how there was very little transition period for this family – they just went from "being without" to being normal and happy, in the veritable blink of an eye. Although she didn't understand it, she did believe that happiness for this family had been fully restored, and she had a longing deep in her heart that she would, one day, feel the same way. When Craig had come back to her, she felt very happy – but not *completely* happy. She desperately wanted that feeling!

As she talked with the other women in her group, she noticed two individuals making their way into the park, from opposite ends. One, a young lady, was someone that she had never met – but knew, oh so well. Diana had made her way into the park, and Addy's emptiness vanished for the day. She settled into the bench on which she was seated and began to watch Diana's movements. While doing so, in a most furtive manner, she began to take more notice of the man who had taken up temporary residence on a bench across from her. She had never seen this man before;

and although he didn't look strange (from a physical standpoint), she felt a sudden chill creep down her spine as a strange and mystical aura seemed to propel the two of them into some tiny, altered universe. When he looked over her way and casually smiled, she smiled back and nodded her head; this made her feel better, putting her a little more at ease.

When the attractive, dark-haired lady had first made eye contact, Whitehouse didn't know what to do; he tried to smile as easily and as naturally as he could, but smiling was not a natural thing for him – being happy was all too new for him to become readily-adjusted to. He leaned back, let the sunlight bathe his face and listened to the birds singing all around him. There were children playing all around. As he watched, a different feeling came over him – one that was unfamiliar. Now, he just sat there and watched them laughing and playing, without a care in the world. He longed to be running around, doing the same things, with other kids his age – and he began to entertain the hope that, one day, he would.

Chapter 21: Business Is Really Booming

Mark and Evan arrived at the same time one morning, and things were already starting to scramble. One of the orderlies, who had gotten there before anyone else, had noticed that one head was already starting to crest, toward the middle of the field. Off to one side, the ground was beginning to shake as four more mounds started to form. When they looked again, they noticed a family standing at the edge of the field, impatiently waiting for someone to tend to them. They also observed a steady stream of people swooping in from all directions.

"What do you think is happening?" asked Mark.

"I don't know, but I have a really bad feeling about this" replied Evan.

The two doctors rolled up their sleeves and immediately dove into their work. As they did, one of the elders (there were always a few located near the harvesting field during the day) summoned a couple of children who had gathered and whispered something to them; then, they took off running in different directions. No one really seemed to notice this happening, because of all the activity on the field, and the swarm of people that now surrounded it.

Evan felt the adrenaline shoot through his entire body. He pulled a couple of people from the crowd and enlisted their help, as did the other doctors. He jumped from one delivery to the next, wiping torrents of sweat from his brow, as he did. The amazing thing was that the harder he worked, the more energized he became; in *Backstep*, you didn't become more tired, you became more full of life. As he pushed ahead, he began to realize this; and yet, the workload was increasing at a very brisk pace – it was difficult to keep up.

Just as he was beginning to wonder how he might manage this situation, a wave of people came to the field; but this group was not coming to claim family members – this group had come to help. Although none of the doctors was aware of this, two of the teachers from the day before, Larry and Bonnie, had told the exact same story – it was a story involving a tremendous silver bird, and a day when lots of people were harvested at the same time – so many, in fact, that the people of the town were called upon to help the doctors. Now, the time had come for the people to be summoned. Larry and Bonnie came too – there were about sixty people in all. They were all prepared; they knew just what to do … and they dove right in.

Mark and Evan couldn't believe what was happening. They were shocked at how skilled these individuals were at being stand-in doctors, and they realized that the teachers had done their jobs well. There was no doubt that the elders of *Backstep* were well prepared for almost any situation, and the citizens were able to step up at almost a moment's notice to deliver what they had to, for the good of the community.

The work continued at a frenetic pace, as ordinary citizens were barking out instructions, just as they had been told to do by their teachers. These were duties they had never performed before, and after today they would probably never do them again; but to them, it wouldn't matter. After seven days, the heat of the moment they were all experiencing, no matter how exciting, would fade into oblivion and would only be revived through the stories that were to be told by the elders. Today proved once and for all how vital storytelling was; one never knew when just the right time would require one to unfold, and bring together the people of the land.

As the bodies continued to be wrapped in purple and stretched out peacefully on the ground, some family members stayed. With the main part of the drama now over, the massive crowd began to thin out; very soon, everyone was gone. No one tried to make sense of it all; it was a wondrous spectacle, which everyone felt drawn to observe. For about three hours, it was utter bedlam; beyond that, life seemed to return to normal. In all, 157 new arrivals had come - all at one time! The doctors and the stand-ins had handled it the way they needed to. Mark surveyed the situation for a moment and started to chuckle. Evan shot him a look of incredulity as he pondered what the gist of the joke might be.

"I was just thinking" said Mark. "It's going to be a heckuva scene one week from tonight when we try to pack all of these families into that dinner hall … we may just have to eat outside."

As he said this, an elder pulled out a pad and pencil and scratched down some notes, for later reference. She did this without calling attention to herself; during the day, the elders tried to operate as stealthily as possible – letting people do their normal activities, but making notes for themselves that they could discuss openly at the Council meetings later in the evening. No doubt, Mark had just said something that provided a spark of an idea that they might put to good use. Citizens contributed to their own learning every day, whether they realized it or not.

"Yeah, that's going to be some kind of big gathering!" Evan agreed.

As he made this comment, he looked around him at all the new arrivals. Gradually, one by one, they were led away to their first lessons and their indoctrination into a new life. The people who were harvested today came in all shapes and sizes … and ages. Most of the people were reasonably young, and they were all uniquely connected through this single event. There were several families that had more than one new arrival; for those families, in particular, the emotions ran extremely high.

Not often, but occasionally, scenes like this unfolded in the land of *Backstep*. In the old world, there were large-scale tragedies that caused many deaths simultaneously; but here, those tragedies were whisked away, and replaced with a feeling of restoration, as puzzle pieces were joined together to make a complete picture once again. None of the population really knew how the system worked; not even the elders were confident that they had an absolutely clear picture of it – but it did work indeed. The elders knew that if they could simply get the citizens to carry on with their normal day-to-day activities and not get caught up in the *hows* and *whys*, things would continue to run smoothly. This is the reason why they so desperately wanted to monitor and control the movements of certain individuals who "colored outside the lines" with their living brushstrokes – and their main focus, right now, was on Craig Alexander.

While his father tended to all the commotion back in the field, Craig was commanding the attention of the children at the hospital. He had never been more popular than he was right now. Although there was still cancer in his system, there was a little less of it with each passing day. His energy level was increasing and his confidence was brimming. He continued to reassure the kids that they could control their own destinies and manage the battle of the disease on their own – through faith and internal will.

"Just do as I do!" he screamed out. He raised a pillow over his head and he swung, clocking one of the nurses on the shoulder. One of the kids laughed, swinging her own pillow and hitting her mother with it.

"Hey!" the woman cried out. She was not expecting the blow, which didn't hurt. When she saw the expression on the little girl's face, the mother's sharp tone quickly changed. She looked over at Craig, smiled and shrugged, and picked up a pillow herself. Before she had any time to react, another pillow hit her from behind. She instantly let out a whoop and turned to swing on her would-be attacker, which just happened to be one of the nurses.

Soon after, the entire wing was filled with children and adults landing shots with down-filled weapons of mass hilarity. Craig saw the joyous mayhem and smiled. These families were no longer thinking about the effects of a disease; they were now turning their attentions to Craig's own brand of medicine which produced an amazing escalation toward a cure: all courtesy of three simple things - time, activity and laughter.

The two elderly women who had been observing Craig for the past few days were captivated by the way he could draw people in with his smile and his carefree mannerisms and then get them to do pretty much whatever he wanted them to do. Even the parents were often charmed by the virtual spell Craig seemed to be able to cast upon them. Their primary concern, of course, was the happiness and well-being of their young ones – many didn't care what great lengths they might have to go through in order to help bring about an ease to the pain and suffering.

"He certainly does have a way with them" one of the women said to the other.

"Well, how could he *not*?" the other questioned. "After all, he has been in their exact same position and everyone knows that … he is showing them the way."

"The way to *what*, exactly?" The taller of the two gazed down her nose at the other, as her demeanor appeared to suddenly grow a little more skeptical and mistrusting. She then continued her mini lecture:

"This is exactly what the Council has tried to warn us about. Even though the young man means well, there is a very real possibility that he could become caught up in his own power and start leading everyone astray … He may be in the process of doing that now!"

"Oh Karen, don't you think you're over-reacting a little?" the more diminutive of the two challenged. "After all, if it's hope he gives them … a little respite from the pain and the physical stresses they are having to endure, not to mention the pressures that their families are having to bear … isn't that worth it?"

Karen looked at Suzanne and studied the lines on her face. "Well, Suzanne … I just don't know what to believe in, sometimes. Here I am supposed to be one of the ones with superior knowledge and reasoning capacity, and yet I find myself falling into the same trap that many others around us have already fallen headlong into – I am almost ready to put my entire faith and trust in this young man, based on what I have seen him do and what I feel deep in my heart."

"I couldn't have said it better myself" Suzanne echoed. "I suppose we should probably keep these things hidden from the Council; otherwise, I am sure that we would be pulled instantly from this assignment… and besides, I still think there are some things we can learn from this young man."

"Yes, yes!" Karen exclaimed. "We will just have to carefully craft our report so that the Council gets what it wants, without revealing too much information or too much sentiment on our part."

"But how are we going to lie to the Council and expect to get away with it?"

Karen thought for a moment and then whispered to her colleague: "You just leave that to me."

Another sunny afternoon found Addy in the park with the rest of her friends. Ivanna, the young mother who had recently added another daughter to her family, was absolutely bubbling with joy. Her two girls were happy, making up games and enjoying all the privileges of childhood. As they continued to talk and watch over the children, Addy noticed a man taking up a spot on one of the park benches. It was the same man she had seen the day before; a cold chill ran down her spine, just as it had the day before.

Craig Whitehouse sat on the same bench he had occupied yesterday; again, all by himself. Today, he was watching children with a new purpose in mind – to learn about what it must be like to laugh and play as a child and to be able to live life in a carefree manner. He was so intent on what he was supposed to be focusing on that it did not occur to him that to be sitting all by himself on the same bench would start to draw other people's attention and make some just a tad bit uncomfortable, perhaps.

One of the people who noticed Whitehouse was Addy. As she watched him, something extraordinary seemed to attract her attention like a magnet;

but she had no idea what the compelling force might be. She supposed that it was due to the fact that he was all alone; and even though she had her own friends around her, Addy felt very much alone herself, right then.

"Should I dare to venture over there and introduce myself?" she wondered.

She only pondered the possible repercussions for a moment or two, before being drawn toward him. She made her way over, to learn a little more about this new stranger in the park. Nervously, she walked over to where he was sitting and made herself sit down as far away as she could, without seeming overly scared or nervous. He noticed her presence, but continued to watch and enjoy the scenery around him.

"Hello" she finally offered. "My name is Addy. I don't recall ever having seen you in this park, before yesterday."

"Yesterday was my first time" the man said. "My name is Craig … hello."

Addy felt several more cold shivers, though she did her best to hide them. "How odd that this man has the same name as my own son!" she thought to herself.

"I have a son - also named Craig" she answered.

The man studied her response. "I've only heard of one other person who has that name: some young kid, battling cancer, who is really making a name for himself over at Childrens' Hospital, I might add."

Addy swelled up with pride. "That's my son" she said. "He returned to me not too long ago, and now he is getting a chance to finally defeat the monster that beat him down for so long in the old world."

"Congratulations!" Craig offered. "I can only imagine how happy it makes you to know that he is doing so much good for so many people." He stopped for a moment, let out a sigh and continued – "I wish that I could do great things that made people happy."

Addy moved in closer on the bench and put a hand on top of his. "You do have a mother, right?"

"Yes, and she is the dearest thing in the world to me!"

Addy fixed a gaze on him that only a loving mother would know. "Was she there when you first arrived?"

"Yes, she was" Craig said, as his eyes started to glisten with moisture.

"Then, strictly from a mother's perspective, I can tell you that you have already made her as happy as you can possibly know. If I could only make you understand the feelings that swept over me when my Craig returned to me – I know they must have been the same feelings your mother felt when you came back to her!"

"I did notice a lot of happy families at that place known as the harvesting field" Craig replied. "Before yesterday, I went there a lot."

"Well then, you probably saw my partner" Addy said, as she began to perk up even more. "He is a doctor in the field ... his name is Evan."

Suddenly, the man on the park bench started to shake. Clutching the hand of his new-found friend a little more tightly, he looked deep into her eyes. She noticed that tears were starting to form behind his greenish orbs as his lips formed the next words:

"Then you are the one I was supposed to find."

Whitehouse went on to explain to Addy how his dreams had directed him to the field on certain days when young children were to arrive. He couldn't remember the exact details of the events that brought him together with those families – those dreams had now faded into darkness and had been replaced by new ones, filled with hope and possibility. As they continued to watch the children, he pointed over toward Rema, and he said:

"That one, over there."

"Yes, what about her?" Addy wanted to know.

"She was the last one ... I remember her face; she arrived just yesterday."

"But I was there" Addy challenged ... "and I didn't see you there. I remember faces very well."

"It's really odd" Craig said, scratching his head. "For some reason, I was directed to the field the day *before* her arrival. To my knowledge, that's the only time that's ever happened. Usually, I would be directed to arrive just prior to the time of the actual deliveries. I could see all the family and friends ... all those people!"

"So you became a divine messenger of some type" Addy reassured him. "Don't you see? In the short time you've been here, you've already helped bring happiness to lots of families – if you are in any way connected with the arrival of their children, you have to be an angel of some sort."

"I guess you're right." Upon hearing Addy's rationalization, Whitehouse felt much better. Way back in the recesses of his mind, the last droplets of horror were vanishing. Never again would he think about or feel the power or dread associated with the former actions of the man who formerly occupied this same body. He was not a rehabilitated man; he was a different man – changing, now, into a caring and loving soul, who had a loving mother and would someday be reunited with a father whose love he had never known.

Addy could feel the relief oozing out of the man, as he continued to shake while sitting on the bench.

"You are among friends now" she told him. "Why don't you come and join us, over there" she offered, as she pointed over to the others.

Craig was unsure, at first. "I'm not really sure" he said. "I don't want to impose or anything."

"Impose?" Addy shot a mock scowl at him and then her expression instantly softened.

"You are a friend of mine now" she said. "And they are all friends of mine, too. One can never have too many of them; and besides, that's what *Backstep* is all about – family and friends."

With that, Addy got up off the bench, offered her hand to Whitehouse, and led him over to where the other ladies sat. Their ring of friendship was about to open, and it was about to accept one more.

Chapter 22: A Bright Light In The Night

Walter didn't like being separated from his grandson. Since his arrival, the two spent as much time together as possible, which wasn't easy. Walter had a demanding teaching schedule, while Craig was busy at the hospital and with his own learning, as well. The old man longed for the day when he could be freed from the shackles of his current workload, and be able to concentrate more on his own family. He was convinced that there were still quite a few things that he could learn from Craig, and wanted to take advantage of all the time they had together before Craig stopped caring and became totally absorbed in childlike routines and behaviors.

Shortly after the time when the sun passed directly overhead, Walter saw a lone figure skipping toward him over the north horizon. The expression on his face softened as he watched his grandson take his place among all the children and adults (some adorned in purple cloaks). Most days Craig got to hear more than one of his stories. Other days, the boy was so busy that he might only make it for one; today happened to be one of those days when sage and young protégé would share only a single opportunity – and they both acknowledged and relished this.

"All right, Wise Walt, what's it going to be today?" Craig asked the question, as the little ones started to scrunch in close around Walter's feet. The old man thought for a moment. Would he tell a story that would benefit and entertain most of his audience? Would he simply see this as a chance to educate his own grandson, and let the others pick up on it as they may? He took a deep breath, gathered his thoughts, arched his back as he sat on top of the ancient story stone, and then began to speak.

Meanwhile, in another part of the village, a young couple sat together in the parlor of their tiny abode, taking turns holding a little bundle of joy. Ellen and Phil Watson knew that there wasn't much time left. For the past seven days, they had experienced absolute joy and perfection with their little boy, to whom they had given the name 'Edward'.

Edward was a helpless infant; he relied totally on his parents – for everything. As one becomes younger and younger in the land of *Backstep*, that's just the way things are. He looked up into their faces; he grinned and gurgled, but did not cry. The tiny eyes glistened, almost as if he knew what was about to happen.

Phil looked at Ellen, and stroked her long blonde hair, as she continued to fixate on the features of the small face and twitching hands.

"I wonder when it will be time to leave?" he voiced.

"I don't know" she answered. "On the one hand, I don't want to leave; but on the other, I know he is about ready – and we need to get on with our lives!"

For many days, a whole lifetime, they had loved and cared for this infant, and now they were following the procedures that would lead to this little one's departure. In actuality, perfection had already been achieved for this boy, except for one final step in the journey. The ritual that they were all about to take part in was nothing special or unique – and it would not dramatically change them for the rest of their lives, although they might remember it for a day or two. This day was all about Edward … and others like him.

As his face continued to glow brighter and brighter, the parents had to eventually shield their eyes. The blinding light continued to pour out, and they knew that the time had arrived for them to take Edward on one last little trip. Wrapping the baby up in a blanket, completely covering him so that they would not be blinded, they began their walk toward the cave – the one that contained the *Light of Pureforth*.

The young couple began the journey, alone; soon, however, two more people joined them, also carrying a tightly-wrapped bundle. This couple was a little bit older, but Phil and Ellen noticed that they bore the same expression on their faces and seemed to walk as if they were in a trance.

Two couples grew to five, then eleven. Not many words were spoken; calm smiles and deep inner reflections were the only means of communication, other than the pressing of flesh, as men and women joined hands in their walk toward a perfect ending for several perfect little beings.

A single file line formed at the entrance to the cave. Ellen and Phil were fourth in line, once they got there. Each time the massive stone door opened, they noticed a wondrous light pouring out and the singing of an angelic choir echoing through the air. Two people, carrying a light blue bundle, entered and then the door sealed behind them. Down a long corridor inside the cave, Ellen could just barely make out what appeared to be a golden altar.

They continued to wait patiently, until it was their turn to enter. Nervousness changed into excitement; the two young people had heard stories about the bright light and the melodious voices, but had never experienced it before, themselves. Now, their time had arrived. The stone door, which looked even bigger up close, slid to the side, beckoning them to enter into the cave. The bright light streamed all around them and the music filled their ears, bathing them in a feeling of utter euphoria. They stepped inside and the door sealed behind them. The music gradually softened and a deep voice boomed:

"Bring the child unto me."

The words echoed all around the walls of the cave. The Watsons looked around, but saw no one. All that they saw, at the end of the long passageway, was a golden crib. The bright light emanated from its center, illuminating the entire cave. Ellen and Phil squinted as they approached, now nearly blinded by the brilliance of the rays. They could make out some of the details of the crib, and noticed that it was lined with softened straw.

Without being told specifically what to do, they placed their bundle in the crib. Upon doing so, a loud chorus of voices sounded harmoniously throughout the cave, and a massive flash of bright light rushed out of the bundle, mixing with the existing light and the sounds that bounced off the walls and ceiling of the great stone temple. When they were able to adjust their eyesight again, the two noticed that the crib was empty – just the way it had been when they entered!

They stood there for a moment, as the light and the music returned to what seemed to be its normal state. The deep voice then said:

"The child has now been received. Edward is now perfect."

With those words, Phil and Ellen turned to exit the cave. Their work was done; they no longer had to worry about their little one. They got to experience the joy that all parents get to witness – the miracle of *childlight*. Some get to experience it more than once; some, one time only. For Phil and Ellen, this was their one and only time. When the door to the cave slid open, they felt free and alive and extremely happy – almost giddy. They saw the expressions on the other faces as they passed back through the line, but they never once looked back. For these two people, life had just reached a new crossroads – now, they could focus most of their attention on each other, and on their parents (both sets of whom had now gathered at the top of the hill). They ran up the hill and collapsed into one big huddle of joy: six family members together, connected only by the streak of perfection that had just exited their world.

After a few moments of rapturous exuberance, the young couple departed, hand in hand, skipping across the fields. They were young and in love, and they had their whole childhoods before them. Their love for each other would eventually fade into a friendship; but for now, they were not thinking about that at all … they were simply enjoying each other's company. In that seminal moment, the two people seemed to grow younger by leaps and bounds, no longer burdened with responsibility.

Two sets of loving parents watched as their children made their way down the hill. Phil's mother, Eunice, squeezed the hand of her partner and said:

"Look at them, Ken. They look so happy and carefree."

"That will be us one day" he reminded her. "As much as we are enjoying our days right now, look at all that we have to look forward to."

Eunice was temporarily absorbed in another thought. "I just can't imagine our Phil as a tiny little bundle like that."

Ken squeezed her hand and pulled her closer. "You don't have to even think about it" he said softly. "Just enjoy each and every day that we have together as a family; that's the lesson they want us to remember and to covet. We must remind ourselves every day, so that we can take advantage of the time we have here in *Backstep*."

"Yes, you're right, of course" Eunice answered, as she leaned over and kissed him on the cheek. "I don't know why, but for a moment there I had this silly notion that this single event would change all of our lives."

Ken nodded. "Well, in a way, I guess it has; but we'll never remember it" he said. "I guess the important things in life are not necessarily the things that you do, but rather who you do them with … I heard that in a story earlier today."

As they faded from the view of their parents, Phil and Ellen approached one of the story tellers. Phil grabbed Ellen by both hands and gazed deeply into her eyes.

"Would you like to hear a story with me?" he asked, with a wry smile.

"Oh yes, I'd love to" she replied. She beamed a great smile, as Phil leaned over and smoothed down a nice spot of grass for her to sit upon. She did so, and looked up lovingly into his face.

"You too" she said, as she patted the ground next to her. Phil eagerly did as he was told, and the young lady looped her arms around his; they snuggled in together, and began to focus on the storyteller. They weren't too late; the story was just about to begin.

Off to the side, a young boy watched as the couple got comfortable. Craig wondered what it must be to be like that – to feel like that. Then, he thought about how full of nonsense it all seemed, and he refocused on the man he admired more than any other – more than his own father, even.

"This is going to be good" he thought to himself. "I wonder what Wise Walt is going to talk about now!"

The old man looked around at his audience. Typically, even after a story started, people would come and go; and yet, it wouldn't matter. For the brief time that they were in his presence, there was a lot of good that he could do for them. Some people were brand new arrivals to *Backstep*, and his voice would be one they would remember for awhile. For others, it was an opportunity to be taught or re-taught a vital lesson. At least one member of his audience would be the protagonist of his story – and wouldn't even know it!

This was the one secret that Walter had shared with his grandson, Craig – the fact that members of the audience were often the lead characters in the stories that were told. Knowing this, Craig had begun to study the various faces in the crowd, trying his best to figure them out. He tried to anticipate which of them was getting ready to have some of the juicy chunks of his or her life sliced open, for all to bear witness to.

"Well everyone ... today, I would like to tell you a story about an extraordinary woman. She wasn't a very large woman (the children snickered when he said this), but she had a very large heart. Her name was Sarah, and she had a boy named Craig."

Craig thought to himself, "Wait a minute! My mother's name is not Sarah!" He felt compelled to interrupt the teacher's introduction; but seeing that impetuous look on the young boy's face, Walter shot him a look that made him freeze where he sat. The look seemed to tell Craig, "You may think you know everything, but you don't!" Even though he never actually said those words, the feeling was communicated rather strongly; and yet, no one else even seemed to notice.

Craig settled back to listen, a little confused. He thought he had this game all figured out; then he thought again:

"Maybe the story *is* about my mother, and he just changed her name."

The more he thought about it, the more details he missed from the story. As is the case with most people during story time, the natural distractions that occur in thought or surrounding sights and sounds cause people to lose track, and they end up missing out on key pieces of information. Fortunately, they don't have to retain any of the particulars or memorize names, facts or dates; many of the stories are ones they will hear again and again – though each time it will be as if they have heard them for the very first time.

Walter continued:

"Sarah was a woman who lived by herself, although she was never alone. Each and every day, she would make her way to the hospital and help take care of special kids. The children she helped out with were special -- not because of anything wrong with them, physically; she helped because these were children whose daddies hadn't arrived yet … the mothers were all by themselves."

"That's so sad" Craig thought. "Could that have possibly been my mother? But wait, it couldn't be … she wasn't by herself … she had dad …"

As Craig continued to work through the puzzle in his head, Walter did not delay the least bit in his delivery.

"Sarah had both a son and a husband, neither of whom she would see for quite a few years; but she always knew that they would return. So, in the meantime, her life's work was bringing smiles and comfort to those women who had children to care for all by themselves.

She established many close friendships; some of these ladies actually drew her in to their own family circles. It was often said that she had so many friends and so many families that she never knew which one she actually belonged to".

Upon hearing this statement, some of the children 'ooohed' and 'ahhhhed', in amazement. Just to think – some people didn't even know who their real families were!

"One of the women, named Trisha, was extremely grateful for the company that Sarah provided her with. They were best friends, and they confided in one another on many matters of the heart, and on raising her little boy, who was named Thomas. He was a very active boy, but he had asthma – so his bouts of wheezing would be followed soon after by lots of running and playing."

By this time, Craig had given up. He had become increasingly frustrated with the fact that, first of all, he didn't know whether this story was about his own mother or not; and secondly, he had already missed enough of the details, due to his own distractions, that he figured it was best now to just sit and be entertained. With that, Craig settled back and relaxed, and began to enjoy the tale – as told by his favorite story teller.

In the land of *Backstep*, some names were called more frequently than others: John, Mary, and Michael, just to name a few. Occasionally, the storytellers would encounter a situation where more than one person of the same name would be in the audience, at the same time. Since they didn't know the stories were actually about them, it didn't cause a lot of angst or confusion. However, on this particular occasion – in this story – the name Craig had come up.

When he first heard his name spoken, Craig's eyes opened wide and he leaned forward. "Certainly, this is about my mother" he thought. "Walter has just tried to cleverly disguise her name, in an effort to throw me off the trail ... but I'm much smarter than that ... I've got it all figured out!"

Walter read the look of triumph on the young boy's face, and he smiled. Craig had just fallen into the trap that the old man had set for him – this was intended to be a *lesson* for him and a *story* for everyone else. He nodded and continued with his story; when he made eye contact with Craig, the young boy felt sure that the ruse had been uncovered. Craig now believed he held the upper hand. He couldn't have been further from the truth!

Sitting off to one side, near the edge of the crowd, was a man in his early thirties. He had a direct connection to Craig's mother, unbeknownst to the young lad. But when the name Sarah was announced as the name of Craig's mother, he instantly knew that the teacher was not referring to the woman known to everyone else as Addy. Instead, he knew that this was a story about his own mother: Sarah. This man's name was also Craig ... Craig Whitehouse.

Chapter 23: Teacher No More

The day began just like every other: calm, bright blue sky, with a few puffy clouds. When Craig got up, he stretched his arms, yawned and set his sights on attacking the day with the same vigor that he always did. His youthful drive seemed to be ratcheted up another notch or two, knowing that the cancerous growth that had been in his body for as long as he could remember was rapidly shrinking. He was not as eager to get to Childrens' Hospital as he had been in the past; he simply wanted to run and play with some of the other kids – the ones who, before now, he had to simply observe.

Shortly after Craig stirred from his sleep, Addy and Evan got up as well. Their days were filled with routine; and although it was the same basic one that they knew so well and had fallen into rather easily, they each noticed that some of the aches and pains they had felt in previous days were going away … it all comes with the territory of growing younger. Evan would soon make his way off to another day of harvesting souls and another night of receiving praise from families he had helped just a few days before. Addy, meanwhile, planned to deliver her son to the hospital, perhaps hear a story or two, then make her way to the park, to join up with friends and enjoy the sanctuary of recreation and relaxation.

What promised to be another day of positive feelings and family unity quickly changed into a morning of frustration for Evan. Shortly after arriving at the field, he became engaged in a struggle with a most unwilling, middle-aged woman, who had long, light brown hair. As he was trying with futility to have her join him on the harvesting plain, she became hysterical. The woman, named Tiffany (but known to all her friends and family simply as "Tiff") was screaming and shaking.

"I can't do this! No, I'm not ready!"

Evan took a deep breath, looked at her calmly, and forced a smile.

"He's waiting for you" were the only words that came out, although Evan wished he had been more clever, and had managed to find the exact right words to do the trick.

Tiff wondered for a brief instant whether or not the doctor knew of her inner turmoil; in fact, all he knew was that she was destined to be reunited with a man named Matthew Burris. He did not know any of the particulars of their past lives or the forces that were drawing them together now. Tiff, however, feeling sudden pangs of guilt as well as being apprehensive toward the life she was ready to step into, was unsure of many things.

Behind Tiff, another man stood, holding her hand. As she reached the height of her emotions, he spun her around, gathered up her hands in his own, and looked deep into her turquoise eyes. His words came easily, but they were also full of impact.

"You must do this" he said. "Our time together has been precious … every single day. But there is someone else waiting for you now, just as there is someone else waiting for me."

As he said this, he nodded toward another woman, standing on a nearby hillside; she was in the middle of a group of people, huddled in close together.

Martin Elliott looked at Tiff, brushed the hair away from her face, wiped away the tear that was streaking down her left cheek, and whispered in her ear that her new, happier life was about to unfold. She didn't understand why he was leaving her now, but a part of her started to be drawn toward the spot where the doctor was beckoning her to join him, for the harvest.

"Go to him now!" Martin directed, as he kissed the woman one last time, then turned and walked away. As he made his way toward the hill, Martin never once looked back at Tiff; his only focus was on the other woman, waiting on the hill.

When Tiff saw this new drama unfold, a stark realization swept over her that her life was suddenly changing. She became cognizant of several of Matthew's family members standing around her – they had been there the whole time, but she had not noticed. One of the family members, an older woman, calmly stepped forward and laid a gentle hand on Tiff's shoulder.

With kind eyes, she looked toward the doctor and smiled slightly. Gently pushing Tiff forward, she said "Doctor, I believe she is ready now."

Tiff felt an odd sensation pulse through her body. Something inside her seemed to release, and she no longer felt vexed by the loss of the long relationship that was now ending with Martin. What she was beginning to realize was that there would no longer be thoughts of, or guilt-ridden associations with, the man who (in a previous life) had stolen her heart and wrecked her marriage. She felt the love swelling in her breast for the man she was about to rejoin. She knew now was the time for her to return to Matthew, and all the family members standing nearby knew the same thing. They all pressed in around her, lovingly and with all the silent support they could offer. In *Backstep*, relationships don't end painfully; they simply melt into others.

The woman sighed and nodded at the doctor; but before she stepped onto the field, she turned around and looked at the man and woman who were Matthew's parents. As she started to speak, the older woman, Jessica, placed two fingers across Tiff's lips and drew her other hand across her cheek. Slowly, and with great depth of feeling, she said:

"What's done is done; you will move on and forget ... we *all* will. Go to Matthew now and have a happy life. Simply let go of what has already passed behind you."

When Jessica said these words, Tiff looked back over her shoulder, toward the hill where Martin had gone; she saw no one – Martin and his whole group had seemingly vanished. Suddenly, there was nothing left for her to ponder or grieve over; now, she felt herself transitioning into a hopeful new stage of her life. She now thought only of Matthew – nothing else. Her heart began to thaw, like the melting ice encasing the fresh waters of a vibrant river, whose currents would then carry her away to happiness.

Tiff finally gave in to her impulses. She looked toward Evan, reached out her right hand, and said the very words that he had hoped to hear:

"Take me to him, doctor ... I'm ready now."

Evan never ceased to be amazed at how quickly peoples' demeanors could change after they arrived at the harvesting field. So many of the faces were ones that he was sure he somehow should recognize, but he could not recall many of them, as he steadily worked day after day. He was only blessed with the ability of piecing families together, although he had neither the insight nor the wisdom to know the intricacies or details of their life stories.

Long before this day, he had given up trying to make sense of the mumblings and musings of the many individuals he had pulled from the ground; he only knew that every story was unique and that it would fade over time – much like his own story. He understood that it was not his place to pry into their personal lives or histories – his role was simply to restore the connections between family members. Once he had accepted this, he had been able to move on, happily, with his own life and family. Fortunately for Evan, this had only required the return of his own son.

Life can be strange. Imagine an empty bag; then envision placing one object in it and picking the bag up to carry it. Day after day, a new object is added, making the weight and the burden that much greater on the bearer. Now, welcome to the land of *Backstep*. In this strange land, all the inhabitants start out with metaphorically heavy bags of build-up from a previous life. Each day, a new (old) item is removed – never to be seen or heard of again by the bearer. Here, people are able to cleanse themselves and escape the throes of remorse and guilt that accompany each and every sin and transgression. Sins are erased, pain goes away, people become younger and more full of vigor – and filled with happiness. It can be a truly wonderful 'rest of your life' – once you accept the fact that perfection looms on the horizon, and there is no use fighting it.

Consequently, there was at least one restless soul in this land who liked to buck tradition and authority: Craig had not eagerly accepted the fact that he was getting younger and stronger, and distancing himself from the condition that had ravaged him from the onset.

He would have preferred to have the cycles reversed – he wanted to view Cancer as a formidable opponent, though time had already shown him that this particular disease (like any other) was easily conquerable … the passage of time was all it took. Craig wanted to be able to challenge diseases head-on in their prime and conquer them – chop them down. He wanted to be able to prove that human spirit and personal will could alter events; he refused to allow himself to cave-in to the prevailing belief and awareness that the natural processes at work in this land determined all outcomes.

"How can I do this?" he thought to himself; and it was a most frustrating predicament for him. What was the point in trying to tackle a monster who was already becoming more and more feeble with each passing day? Where would the feeling of triumph be, in the end? Craig did not know why he felt so conflicted and so out of step with almost everyone else in *Backstep*, but he relentlessly continued in his own personal quest to solve mysteries on his own – even if it meant ostracizing himself from the mainstream of society, at times.

The young man surveyed the situation around him. All the children in the hospital had been eagerly anticipating his arrival, and were excited about the new games or surprises he might have in store for them. As he snapped back into reality, Craig knew that he was now the ringmaster and that the show was about to begin. Like always, he really planned to let loose!

Craig knew that he was being watched and scrutinized as he interacted with the kids from the "gradual progression" ward (the place where the sickest kids were placed). Almost all were very sick upon their arrival, but were gradually getting better. Much of the credit for their increasing wellness was simply the reversal of time and its ability to gradually restore good health – and youth. But as Craig moved here and there, starting up games and "stirring up trouble" among the nurses and staff, all the kids began to forget about their own limitations and personal setbacks. Some observers began to actually believe that young Craig possessed a certain aura that no one had ever seen before – he certainly had the stuff of which leaders are made. He was so revered, that many thought of him as a sort of "boy king". This was the very notion that brought concern to the elders.

The twelve-year-old continued to battle through his own physical pain as he grabbed a cane out of a stand next to one of the nurse's stations. Holding it high in the air, he kicked his head back and yelled at the top of his lungs:

"We're going to have a parade!"

He ran over to a young girl who was slumped forward in a wheelchair, and placed the cane across her lap. Turning around swiftly, he pointed at her and cried out:

"…and here's our leader!"

The girl, Irene, raised her eyes; they flashed like diamonds in the sun. A wide smile spread across the place that had formerly been occupied by sadness and despondency. How could Craig have possibly known that a parade was exactly what this little girl both wanted and needed? Whether he knew it or not, giving her the chance to lead the line down the hall would provide Irene with a kind of ecstasy that no elixir could ever come close to producing.

Craig jumped behind Irene's wheelchair and announced:

"We're going down G, H and I halls … who's with me?!"

Naturally, his command prompted an almost immediate response:

about two dozen sick children either walked on their own, wheeled themselves, or clamored for the assistance of other people to help them line up and prepare for the journey down the pre-determined parade route.

Craig demonstrated to others how to wave to the crowd. He barked instructions to several of the staff members to blow up balloons or to scrawl out a couple of crude, makeshift banners for the children to hold up as they marched down the halls. The children lined up, eager for the announcement to begin: parents leaped behind wheelchairs; others supported boys and girls on feeble, yet determined, limbs.

Word quickly spread throughout the wing of the hospital; G, H and I halls were teeming with anticipation. It had been almost a week since the last parade. Some of the newer arrivals had never witnessed one before; others could just barely recollect. Parents in the rooms along the route prepped sick young boys and girls about what they were about to see and experience. The entire place was abuzz with exuberance and high expectations.

"Here we go!" the grand master yelled. Craig pulled a kazoo out of his pocket, shoved it into the side of his mouth and began an impromptu tune that sounded like nothing in particular. Other kids began to cry out for their own kazoos; soon, the hallways were filled with the chaotic sounds of Craig's band of merrymakers. It was a marked contrast from the sterile, almost gloomy environment that formerly resided there.

If there was any doubt at all as to the validity of this "medicine" conjured up for many by a simple young boy, it was quickly dispelled. As they made their way down the hallways, each marcher paused at every doorway, catching the glimpse and the smile of a child too sick and weak to move from his or her own bed. The participants in the parade marched and waved, accompanied by banners, pictures and balloons. They were able to bring joy to each and every child along the route – the sick children in their beds turned their hopeful faces, showing what little expressions of thanks they could offer in return.

Once the parade was fully under way, Craig got someone else to replace him behind Irene's chair. The little girl did not seem to care in the least as another attendant took his place … she was "in charge" and that was all she cared about at the moment! Craig ran up and down hallways, letting the residents of G, H and I know what was coming (of course, by then, everyone was fully aware). Everyone was in an uplifted mood; and not just the children … parents, nurses, other family members, volunteers and staff members were all in on the act – and what an act it was!

As the others cavorted around, two people watchfully took in the scene, studying the celebration carefully. On the one hand, they wanted to applaud the initiative and spirit displayed by the boy known as Craig. They couldn't help but notice the sphere of influence he had created for himself. The two women chatted with each other, not sure at first whether to be more impressed or more intimidated.

"Rose, what is it exactly that makes this boy such a threat to our society?"

"I don't really know, Elizabeth" said her companion. "It was explained to us that this young man, Craig, has a certain ability to manipulate other peoples' minds and actions, which could potentially threaten the order of life as we know it."

"But I just don't see it in him" countered Elizabeth. "What I *do* see is someone who is more concerned about the happiness and well-being of others than he is even of himself."

Rose said, "Yes, I see that too; however, the warning comes due to the fact that he is getting younger and stronger day by day, and he *knows* this – he *feeds* off this – and the number of followers is growing."

"But how can this be? If life is working backwards, wouldn't people eventually forget about him, and stop caring?"

"It's not that simple" Rose bristled. "Don't you remember what they told us at the Council meeting? Look, all we have to do is report what we see back to the other elders. I am glad we are only here for five more days. It will get better each day, until we're done."

"I'm looking forward to being done, too" agreed Elizabeth. "Personally, I think this is a worthless exercise. All I see is a harmless little boy."

"Unless …" Rose started to roll the possibilities in her mind, as she thought through what she was about to verbally unveil. "Unless that's exactly what he *wants* us to think! Could it all just be an act to get all the adults around him to simply prop him up as some kind of savior for the people?"

Elizabeth scratched her head and studied the words she was about to say next. "What could he possibly save anyone from -- growing younger and stronger? Please! He can't alter the natural progression of time. What can one person do?"

Rose nodded, obviously succumbing to the propaganda that had been pumped into her constantly, before taking on this little spying venture. "I understand that he wants people to believe in the power of their own individuality. He wants people to feel like they can control their own destinies and overcome the restrictions and limitations placed on them by the reverse passage of time."

"And all this comes from the people making all the rules and laws, right?" Elizabeth questioned.

"Yes!" snapped Rose. "The elders know what is best. They – we – are not often challenged; but anytime someone new is discovered who tries to upset the natural order of things, he (or she) must be dealt with quickly and diplomatically. Otherwise, it could pose a danger to everyone!"

Elizabeth thought about Rose's words and began to reconsider the nature of their task. "If all we've got to do is observe and report, I guess there's not really much point in worrying about anything else. I wonder what we might be able to learn from him, in the meantime."

"Elizabeth, it is NOT OUR JOB to try and learn anything from him!" Rose snapped. "He is only a boy; and *we* are the teachers – don't you remember?"

Elizabeth noted how her friend and colleague had become extremely irritated and was beginning to treat the subject of their research as a true threat to the entire population of *Backstep*.

"Rose, why are you acting this way? What has this boy done wrong?" she wondered aloud.

"Well, he hasn't done anything wrong … yet; but the concern is that he *might* do something."

"What do you think he *might* do?" Elizabeth asked.

"I think he might work to replace the existing set of rules and laws that we have come to accept without question … he could be the archangel of anarchy!"

"I don't get that feeling when I watch him" said Elizabeth.

"What either of us gets is of no concern" Rose answered. "The only thing that matters is what the Council interprets and decides upon as its next course of action."

With that, Rose closed the book on the discussion between the two elderly colleagues. They continued to silently watch as the parade concluded, giving way to other games, and followed later by story time. This last part was what concerned the elders the most: this was when the children would all gather around Craig and listen to him weave a tale of wonder. Craig was a master at capturing peoples' attention and he was a truly gifted wordsmith – especially for someone his age. Could it be that he was, in fact, a better storyteller and a more accomplished teacher than those who were the already-established rank-and-file instructors – much, much older than himself?

Craig's story seemed harmless enough; but the women who studied him were more interested in how he interacted with his audience. When he finished, he quietly gathered his belongings and silently stole out the back door of the hospital. He was eager to hear a story or two from his own grandfather; after all, this was Walter's last day as a teacher. After today, there would be no more chances to share in his collective wisdom.

As Craig made his way to his grandfather's familiar hill, he began to think about what the coming days and years would mean for him. Tomorrow would almost seem a little awkward because Walter would no longer be an esteemed teacher or elder. Craig loved his grandfather and held him in the highest regard – and with utmost respect. However, once Walter was no longer a teacher – an elder – how might their relationship change? Craig wondered about this and became slightly troubled, as he slowly trudged up the hill where Walter and his adoring public had gathered. Craig didn't usually worry about too much; today, however, his head swirled with conflicting thoughts. He desperately hoped that the story he was about to hear would help him decide what to do next in his young life.

Chapter 24: Now, It's Time To Live

For Walter, as he rolled out of bed and stretched his arms at the start of a new day, some things felt somewhat different. Flexing his muscles, he noticed that some of the familiar aches were gradually going away. He seemed to be able to frame his own thoughts a lot more clearly. His mind was able to push trivial things aside more readily, and his eyesight seemed to be improving. In the Council meetings, he had been told that all these things were a pleasant side-effect of growing younger, and even though he had noticed it all around him every day for as long as he could remember, only now did he truly start to believe.

As he prepared himself for the trek to his familiar story-telling post, Margaret joined him for a light breakfast of yogurt and a strange kind of hardened bread, topped with strawberry preserves. He did not remember ever having this for breakfast before. Walter asked his partner about this and she explained how the Council had delivered these things the night before – that *this* was the traditional breakfast served to those who would be teaching for the final time.

"They say that it's a 'time-honored tradition'" Margaret explained. "The yogurt represents the 'milk of life' that you will eventually take from your mother, before you depart this land. The hardened bread represents your arrival, and it's topped with the sweet, thick juiciness of all the things yet to come. Since I was never a teacher myself, I can only believe that what they say is true." She said this with a smile and a wink.

Walter paused for a moment. Of course, she was right. When Margaret had first arrived, she was already too young to be a teacher; it was a special privilege for Walter. It was a unique bond that could only be experienced by a few people in his family – only those who lived long lives in another world would ever know what it was like to teach others in this one. He took a bite of the yogurt and ripped an edge off of the hard bread with his teeth.

"Is there anything special I'm supposed to think or feel while I'm eating this breakfast?" he asked.

"I don't really know", Margaret responded. "I guess it has some significance, but since they didn't say anything more, it must be another one of those 'riddles' that you have to solve on your own."

Ah yes, the 'riddles'! As far back as he could remember (which was about four years; the elders were able to retain things much longer than those under eighty), members of the Council would occasionally be faced with perplexing situations that they would have to mull over, make sense of, interpret to each other, and then etch into the lore that surrounded the society. They did this by creating stories. Many that were told by members of the Council came about as a result of these memorable events. Walter almost hated not to be a part of this any longer. However, as he was becoming younger, he was noticing that he didn't have as much of an appetite for it as he used to. Besides that, the issues that had been coming up were much more frequent and they seemed to always revolve around Craig.

Since his arrival, Craig had really become a thorn in the sides of most of the Council members. It wasn't that they disliked him, but it was evident that his dreams often conflicted with their visions of how things should be (and how things should be taught). Some discounted his musings as that of a young boy whose mind was still wracked with the delusional tendencies associated with the disease that his body was fighting off. Others however, viewed him as a danger – a threat to the order and stability that the Council had fought so hard to maintain over the land and its people.

Walter became amused when he thought back to instances when Craig had embarrassed more than one teacher by contradicting his (or her) story, then breaking into a story of his own. It was quite unusual for a boy to even think of himself as a teacher! Many didn't seem to mind; some rather enjoyed it. There were a few leaders, however, who bristled at the very idea that one person (a boy, at that) could come in and upset an entire culture, an entire tradition - one story at a time.

Even though Craig rarely bothered Walter, he could understand why some of the Council leaders felt the way they did. He began to understand more and more that Craig's daily appearances at the hospital for sick children came as more than just a coincidence … it was also a way of isolating him from the teachers. It was a way for the Council to control the way things happened day in and day out. Walter was rather glad to be stepping away from all this, even though he knew that for the rest of his days here, his own life would be controlled by decisions to which he would no longer have a say.

As he finished his breakfast and began the journey to his familiar perch, Margaret kissed him on the cheek and wondered aloud: "Have you decided on what stories you are going to tell today?"

"Well, I thought I might tell the story of John, the fisherman, once again (it was one of Walter's favorites) and then perhaps a tale about my cousin Reginald (who was now about fifty-five years old and working hard every day as a vegetable gardener, but who used to be one of the most beloved teachers of all time) … but the story I really want to be able to tell, just one more time, is the story of Margaret!"

His partner blushed as he said this; in that moment, they both realized that their lives together would start to change after this day was over. "Would it be alright if I came along and heard you on your final day?"

"Why, I would be honored, my dear", he offered thoughtfully. "I can't think of anyone I would rather spend time with!"

"Well, after today, it looks like we will finally be able to capitalize on that time together that you have spoken of so frequently" she added.

The couple cleaned up their breakfast dishes, tidied up their small hut, and then made their way to the place where stories would unfold and where culture was repeated over and over into the heads of the children – memories that would all be wiped away in just seven days' time. Walter wondered what living without a collective memory would be like; at the same time, he knew he was fortunate to have even had this opportunity. Being able to teach was a gift; a gift reserved only for the very old. Very soon, this gift would have to be exchanged for the chance to live the rest of his life.

Evan and Mark continued to enjoy their own repetition of work, family, and nightly dinners. Life in *Backstep* had its routines and its structure, but it seemed fairly fluid. Nothing significant had happened, of late, to dramatically alter their world. However, on one particular day, everything changed.

When Evan got up one Sunday morning, he felt eerie; he thought that he heard the sounds of angel voices swirling around him. He had heard them once or twice before, and it usually indicated that he was about to perform a very important harvest. He tried to brush away the buzzing in his ears, but it stayed with him all the way to the Field.

Once he got there, he caught up with Mark, who was banging the side of his head with the heel of his hand.

"Ears ringing?" he asked Mark.

"Yes! It started kind of low this morning, but it has grown steadily all morning long."

"Mine too!" Evan admitted. "I wonder what it all means."

As the two friends and colleagues tried to make sense of what they were feeling, they both began to tremble. At almost the same moment, they noticed a collection of people beginning to assemble from every end of the Field. It would turn out to be the most massive gathering that anyone in the land could ever remember — even among the elders.

There were no family members to greet the two doctors. Stunned at first, they felt themselves drawn to the exact center of the harvesting grounds. As Evan began to get all the supplies together that they would need, Mark looked over his shoulder and began barking orders at one of the assistants.

"Get four large sheets and a white cloak!" he yelled.

As people began scurrying and filling Mark's orders, his friend looked at him quizzically.

"Where did those orders come from?" asked Evan.

"I don't know … somewhere deep within me, I guess. It's like I'm in charge, but I'm not really in charge. Whoever we're getting ready to harvest … all I can say is … this is pretty monumental!"

The two men quickly and seriously conducted their business. Sheets were put up all around them, to project a sense of awe and intensity, as well as privacy. The doctors ducked inside the sheets, and a contemplative hush rolled across the countless masses.

After what seemed like an interminable wait, one figure emerged from the walls of white sheeting. Wearing a shimmering white cloak, a man slowly strode a few paces from the drapery, which now fell around him. His face was worn and cracked, but his eyes shined like brilliant sapphires. He directed his gaze toward the west side of the Field, where a large group of elders had gathered.

"It's him! It's Abraham!" The words cascaded throughout the crowd. Teachers had been preparing the good folk of *Backstep*. The leadership had anticipated this one true figure — the one who would lead them to a new sense of peace and direction, and serve as a living, breathing symbol of all the hope that was theirs to come.

The old man looked all around him, slowly arched his head backward and extended his arms as far out to his sides as he could reach.

"I am Abraham of Backstep!" he loudly announced. "Bless you all!"

With those words, he made his way to the group of elders, who instantly cocooned him and led him toward the cave in which all the highest and most sacred meetings took place on a nightly basis. Abraham was escorted to the House of the Council, a place he would very rarely leave over the course of the next twenty or so years. He would soon be installed as the new Council Chief and the laws of society would form around whatever he might happen to dictate. The elders had waited for the arrival of this man; many had prayed for it. Now, the moment had arrived and there was a single person who could be looked upon for stable leadership, over a long period of time.

The crowd began to disperse, as the trail of men and women dressed in an array of brightly-colored cloaks disappeared from sight. The bright white luminescence of Abraham shone from the center of the mass. As the Council made its way over the hill, the two doctors stood side-by-side, suddenly alone in their little world of harvesting.

"How old do you think he is?" Mark asked.

"I don't know" replied Evan. "Now, it's time to live – for him, anyway. And, I guess, for *all* of us. But I have this sneaking suspicion that things around here are about to change!"

On another hillside, far away from the harvesting field, Craig was on a secret personal mission. He had been listening to the stories of his grandfather, on Walter's final day as an elder, but he had become restless and quietly removed himself from the group, seemingly undetected. He had heard stories about the cave that contained the *Light of Pureforth*. He clearly understood that it was the place to go when bodies of this world were ready to be welcomed into a state of eternal perfection. Only infants who shone with the bright light were able to be transported – their families would carry them to the cave, deliver them to the light, and that was that.

But Craig wanted to know why. "How does it all work?" he wondered.

"What would happen if I stepped into that light? I've already been told that I can't die; so what *would* happen?

Every member of Craig's family would have done their best to pull him back, if any of them had known what he was planning. His intentions were not in the least bit mean-spirited, but his actions could impact an entire society.

As he stood behind a rock near the entrance to the cave, he carefully watched the eyes of all the people who carried the brightly-shining bundles. He studied their eyes, their movements, and tried to pay close attention to the words they spoke. In the end, he didn't come away with much.

"I've just got to stay still and wait for the right moment" he thought to himself. "I just have to be patient!"

Finally, as nightfall creeped in, the end of the line of people making their perfect little deposits made their way into the mammoth cave. He presumed that as soon as the last person was out, the door to the cave would close. Craig readied himself for his next move. He felt his body tense as the final couple made its way closer to the massive entrance.

As soon as they exited, a rock began to move, closing the entrance. Without hesitation, Craig ran inside and hid behind a rock along the wall, just as the stone door slammed shut.

Craig double-checked; there was no one else around. An eerie humming noise echoed about the walls of the cave, and he was both excited and frightened about what he had impulsively decided to do.

Turning to face the deep corridor of the cave, he saw an extremely bright light ahead of him. He didn't know how long the passageway was; the light was so bright, it distorted his view. Craig held a hand in front of his face to shield his eyes, and began to make his solitary, and quite forbidden, short trek toward the *Light of Pureforth*.

Photo by Ross Bosse

F. Thomas Jones, a native of North Carolina, lives in northern Virginia where he teaches English at the middle school level. He is an avid sports fan, enjoys all types of music (especially jazz and blues) and loves spending time with his family.